WILD FRONTIERS

NINE STORIES OF THE WEST

WILD FRONTIERS

NINE STORIES OF THE WEST

Commissioning Editor

Jeffery L. Blehar

And featuring stories by

Kevin M. Folliard

Misha Burnett

Jackson Kuhl

J. Conrad Matthews

Damito Huffman

Stephen Coghlan

Patrick Winters

Dave Higgins

CONTENTS

INTRODUCTION

The wide open spaces of the West, filled with freedom and danger in equal measure, where a person might forge a destiny by the strength of their own hand or hide from a life gone off the rails.

As a child, I lived in a two-bedroom bungalow. Like most children, I went through a period of waking up early. Normally, I'd go into the living room to watch television. However, because we lived in a two-bedroom bungalow, whenever we had overnight guests someone would be sleeping on the sofa and I'd have to stay in my room quietly until a more sociable hour. So, I read in my room. I had plenty of books but I kept returning to a stack of illustrated annuals (the precursor of the graphic novel); there were some classics in there (Robin Hood, Ivanhoe, &c.) but many of them were cowboy stories.

Working through them one-a-morning for the duration of my grandparents' stay, I must have read them all every Christmas for years. I was too young to properly understand some of the nuances, especially any romantic tension there might have been, but those stories held my attention even after all that rereading.

As I got older, my tastes broadened; but there was always something about the archetypal cowboy tales that I came back to. Watching reruns of *Rawhide* while I ate lunch. Staying up until the early hours of the morning to watch *The Good, the Bad and the Ugly* again.

My reading (and certainly my own work) is mostly speculative these days: I'm more likely to read *The Dark Tower* than *Lonesome Dove*, watch *Wynonna Earp* than *Gunfight at the OK Corral*. But the forays into the limitless opportunity of the Old West are still going on.

So, while the leather waistcoat and gun belt I got when I was six don't fit me any more, when I heard Jeffrey was looking for submissions for an anthology of Westerns, I wanted to add my own (slightly weird) voice to the campfire. When I later discovered he also needed a publisher for the project, I saddled up and vowed to bring the project home.

Fortunately, it's not a ride I need to take alone.

Kevin M. Folliard's "Hangman's Knot" introduces us to Bobby, a woman outside the law but still dishing out a sort of justice.

In Misha Burnett's "Mystery Train" what should be a simple escort job becomes a nightmare and a man who isn't as good as he could be discovers he might be as good as he needs to be.

Jackson Kuhl's "Llano Estacado" takes us back to a time when the Mexican border was still in flux and asks what a man might do if his land changes nations overnight.

Superstition battles common decency in J. Conrad Matthews' "Dusk Woman", the tale of a traveling blacksmith who can't let children suffer just because they're natives.

Damito Huffman's "Josephine's Revenge" reminds us that a decent woman pushed too far can be more dangerous than any outlaw.

Stephen M. Coghlan's "Such is the Nature of the Change" takes us to a future where the lawless frontier has come again and shows that the gunslinger spirit will live on as long as one person is prepared to take a stand.

In Patrick Winter's "Absolution", a simple visit to a saloon becomes a eulogy for the loss of the Old West.

And "The Amarillo Job", a self-contained extract from Jeffery L. Blehar's own novel *Devlin*, brings us the classic tale of a mysterious traveler drawn into the problems of a isolated town.

I hope you enjoy them as much as I do.

—Dave Higgins, 19 March 2019

Hangman's Knot

Kevin M. Folliard

Late afternoon, the town square was all but deserted. Daniel Kenny was on his way to Hackshaw's Saloon when he spotted a lone rider on the horizon. He fingered the handle of his six-shooter. The rider wore a tan hat and red bandanna over the face. Daniel's grip relaxed as the figure drew nearer, and a tight denim shirt revealed that this rider was a lady.

Her white horse trotted into town. She dismounted and guided the stallion to a trough.

Daniel approached. The rider's blond ponytail swished beneath her hat as she cooed to her horse and led him away from the water. She wound the reins haphazardly around the post outside the bank.

Daniel smiled. He reached for her.

The woman craned her neck around and flashed stern gray-green eyes. "Mind those hands, boy."

"Didn't mean nothin'." Daniel raised his hands in mock surrender. "Can't a gentleman help a lady tie her horse up proper?"

"No. I mean watch those hands, mister gentleman, sir." Her horse snorted, stamped a hoof. "This one bites."

"I've been known to tame a few wild ones." Daniel tipped his hat and extended his hand. "My name's Dan Kenny. Folk call me Danny. How do you do?"

The woman ignored him. She pulled a fistful of grains from her saddle bag.

Daniel lowered his hand. "Got a name, lady?"

She laughed. "Lady'll do."

"Okay, lady. Why cover that pretty face?" He gestured to the red bandanna "Ain't that dusty out there."

"So sure I'm pretty?"

"I got a hunch you ain't a crone."

She pulled the kerchief down to her neck, revealing silken skin, a round face, and spritely smile. "Happy? Now, if you don't mind, I got business." She nodded at the bank. "You keep your money there, son? Or in your piggy bank?"

"I haven't told you how old I am."

"I got eyes, junior."

Daniel beamed. "I got money, lady."

"Your paw gives an allowance, huh?"

"You've got some lip." His smile broadened. He rubbed his chin. "I like that. You from out west?"

"Out west?" Her horse lapped up oats from her hand.

"You passed through Ridgewood, I'm guessing. I rode that way once with a friend. Had a fine time at Ms. Fennel's house."

"You've mistaken me for a different kind of lady, Danny boy. Is it because I'm pretty? Because I ride by my lonesome? Or did angels stamp the word 'Trollop' on my forehead while I wasn't paying attention?"

The boy wrung his hands, blushed. "I'm not making judgements."

"Smartest thing you've said so far." She patted her horse. "Now run along, little boy."

Danny blocked her path. "Bank's open another hour at least, miss. I do have money on me. Could make that deposit a little bigger."

She leaned close, tapped Danny's cheek. "I'm here to make a *withdrawal*, cowboy."

"May I add to your withdrawal?"

"You have nothing I want."

"There's a room," he whispered. "Back of the church. Nobody uses it. Wouldn't take long."

"Mister Gentleman." The woman reached behind her back. "I am going to have to ask you to move."

Daniel Kenny smiled. He took a step forward, forcing the woman to tilt her head up at him. He grabbed her shoulders. Pulled their hips together. "Not such a little boy after all, am I?" he growled. "I have a gun. And it is loaded. And my father is the law around these parts. So just join me in the back of church, for a few minutes. I promise, you will enjoy it as much as I will."

The woman scowled. "All I needed was a reason, Danny the Gentlemen."

A sharp, wet sound sliced between them. Pain flared in Danny's guts.

"Thank you for providing one."

"Raise 'em, lady!" Sheriff Tom Kenny's finger itched the trigger of his six-shooter. After tracking Roberta "Bandit Bobbi" Hawkins all night across Jade River into the caverns under Jackknife Mesa, he finally had her. Cool damp air washed over them. Bat squeaks echoed in distant shadows.

Bobbi's boots shuffled grit as she turned and held her hands high. "You caught me, Sheriff. Put that away; I'll come quiet." She cocked her head. Her ponytail swished.

"Not a chance." With his free hand, Kenny unfastened a coil of rope from his belt.

"This is no way to treat a lady." Bobbi giggled, the same girlish laugh the Sheriff figured she'd used on his sixteen-year-old son Daniel, before she'd knifed him, stolen his gun, and left him to die, face down in the horse trough.

Immediately afterward, Bobbi robbed the bank and rode away under a pink sky.

"You're no lady," Kenny growled. "Turn around. Hands in the air."

Bobbi complied. Sheriff Kenny approached with caution. He pushed his gun against her back, patted Bobbi's sides with the other hand. He relieved her of her belt and holster, two guns including Danny's, and a throwing knife she kept strapped to her ankle.

"Hands behind your back." The Sheriff tapped her with his revolver.

"Most ungentlemanly, Sheriff." Bobbi lowered her arms.

The Sheriff bound Bobbi's wrists.

"Mind the circulation in my wrists, Sheriff."

Kenny yanked Bobbi out of the cavern.

"I'll be sure to inform the jury how rough you were when you cornered and bruised a pretty thing like me."

"You do that." Kenny jammed the gun in Bobbi's back as they entered the sunlit plateau. "Get up."

Bobbi squinted at the Sheriff's horse. "I can't mount your steed with hands behind my back."

"Then I'll drag you through the dust."

Bobbi chuckled. "I brought out the devil in you, didn't I, Sheriff?"

"Get up."

Bobbi approached the horse. "Y'all will have to help me."

Kenny steadied her as she mounted his horse. He climbed on behind her.

"What if I fall?" Bobbi said.

Kenny reached around her and grabbed the reins. "You'll get hurt." They galloped across the desert toward Jade River. The wind knocked Bobbi's hat away. Golden hair whipped behind her. Sun scorched her face.

"Did you find my horse?" Bobbi asked. "He all right?"

"You have the nerve to ask about your beast?"

"My horse didn't hurt nobody. Didn't steal from your bank. Just wondering."

Kenny's voice came out like ice. "Keep wondering."

They galloped on in silence. Dust devils twirled across the horizon; tumbleweeds made lazy cartwheels across the desert. As the sun began to set, Bobbi sang:

Hangman, hangman,
slack your rope awhile.
I see my daddy comin'
ridin' many miles.
Daddy, bring your silver.
Or bribe him with your gold.
Unless you want your girlie
A'hangin' from the pole!

"Such a pretty voice," the Sheriff growled.

"I say thank you, Sheriff!" Bobbi shouted. "I don't plan to go to the gallows myself, though. I plan to make a nice life, on a ranch someplace."

"That so?"

"I know you loved your son, Sheriff. But he attacked. I defended myself. Folk'll see it that way."

Kenny's horse approached Jade Bridge.

He slowed, pulled sideways, and galloped up shore.

"That's not the way to town." Bobbi slowly worked a pair of sewing scissors from inside her sleeve, past her wrists. She maneuvered the handle into her fingertips. She had half a mind to jam them into the Sheriff's thigh, but not yet. Instead, she sawed the ropes, frayed the Sheriff's knot.

They galloped upriver until the serrated tips of gray fenceposts jutted over the horizon. The curved façade of a wood perimeter loomed west of the river. A crumbling staircase dangled from a log lookout tower, and a tattered Union flag whipped atop a flagpole.

"This don't look like justice, Sheriff."

"It is to me."

Bobbi clenched her scissors as Sheriff Kenny dismounted.

"This fort's been abandoned for years. I'm gonna tie you to the flagpole and let the wolves have you." He guided his horse toward the entrance.

Bobbi furiously worked at the rope. "A man of the law shouldn't be in this situation. Take me back. Lock me up."

"I considered that." The Sheriff pushed open the wooden gates. Rusty hinges creaked. "But I've heard tales of Bandit Bobbi's silver tongue. Why take chances?"

The horse trotted between the thick support posts of an arched opening. Darkness loomed in the broken windows of a collapsed barracks. Somewhere amid stacks of wood-rotted debris, a rattlesnake shook its cold warning.

Bobbi picked and snipped at the frayed knot. "What about the money, Sheriff? Don't you want to know where I hid it?"

"You killed my son. That money can stay lost forever for all I care."

"I ain't a good girl, but it was self-defense."

Sheriff Kenny halted. He turned and set chill blue eyes into Bobbi's.

She held her scissors stiff behind her.

"I would take Danny here, when he was still small enough to ride with me. I'd show him this fort, tell him war stories. Watch his eyes grow wide as teacups. He loved those stories." The Sheriff's hand cradled his holster.

10

"But more than anything, he loved to hear about his momma. The woman who died giving life to our only child. My wife was a good girl. Now she has no legacy."

"I am deeply sorry for that loss, Sheriff." Bobbi nodded with understanding. "Your little gentleman would have benefited tremendously from a mother's discipline."

The Sheriff scowled and drew his revolver. "Get off."

Bobbi tucked the scissors in her palm and slid onto the ground. The horse snorted. A cloud of dust ghosted through the fort's interior.

"Stand by the flagpole."

Bobbi marched to the pole. She glanced back and spotted Kenny retrieving a second coil of rope. She faced the pole and waited.

Kenny grabbed Bobbi's neck. In the moment when she imagined he needed two hands to uncoil the rope, she stabbed back with her scissors.

Blood spurted. The Sheriff shouted, "Bitch!"

Bobbi twisted around and kneed his groin. She kicked the hand that held the revolver just as he fired. The bullet rang against the flagpole. The horse whinnied.

"Evil bitch!" His voice wheezed.

The revolver landed in the dust.

Kenny grabbed Bobbi's throat and banged her head against the pole. Double-vision split the Sheriff's wild eyes into four. Bobbi struggled to break the rope. She hadn't frayed the knot enough.

"I'll choke the life out of you!"

Bobbi pressed against the pole for leverage. She kicked the Sheriff's knee, and his grip loosened. Bobbi charged him with her shoulder and tackled him to the ground. She bit his fingers. Hot, metallic blood pooled under her tongue.

The Sheriff wrenched away. His bloody fingers clutched his stomach.

Bobbi felt something hard underneath her—the barrel of a pistol, by the small of her back. She wriggled her body, worked her fingers around the cold metal handle.

"I'll kill you!" Kenny lurched forward, ice blue eyes wide and monstrous. "Kill!"

She somersaulted, squeezed the trigger. Gunfire cracked. She squeezed a second and third time. Twin pops vibrated like thunder from her fingertips. Gunpowder lingered in the air. Bobbi flipped onto her feet and turned around.

Kenny's knee was blown out, his shirt soaked red. His jaw slackened to a half-sung word: "Daaa—aa—y . . ."

"Sorry, Sheriff." Bobbi dropped the revolver and headed to the scissors by the flagpole. She picked them up and worked at the knot. "Sorry you raised a pig." The knot snapped, and the ropes plopped on dusty ground. Bobbi retrieved the Sheriff's gun.

Tom Kenny's gaping mouth struggled and shook. His eyes went glassy.

Bobbi stole his hat; mounted his horse.

"You know something, Sheriff?" She tipped her hat. "You look just like your son."

She spurred the horse through open gates, beneath a pink sky. More than anything, Bobbi wished to ride back to town—where she prayed the horse she had loved for two long years waited—wished she could swap the Sheriff's horse for hers. But she was no fool.

She could love this horse too.

"Ride, beautiful, ride!" She worked the horse into a gallop.

Kevin M. Folliard is a Chicagoland writer whose published fiction includes scary stories collections *Christmas Terror Tales* and *Valentine Terror Tales*, as well as adventure novels such as *Matt Palmer and the Komodo Uprising*. His work has also been collected by *The Horror Tree, Flame Tree Publishing, Hinnom Magazine*, and more. Kevin currently resides in La Grange, IL, where he enjoys his day job as an academic writing advisor. When not writing or working, he's usually reading Stephen King, playing Street Fighter, or traveling the USA.

Mystery Train

Misha Burnett

"Did you see much action during the war, Mr. Moriarty?" Isaiah Cotton, the Salt Lake City stationmaster asked.

Sean Moriarty frowned. "If you're referring to the War Between the States, sir, I was thirteen years old in '65."

The old man raised bushy white eyebrows. "Thirteen in '65... that would make you thirty-one today?"

"Yes, sir," Moriarty agreed.

"You look older than that," Mr. Cotton said. "Where are you from?"

"Illinois, sir. Town of Wood River."

"A Yankee, then."

"I prefer to think of myself as an American."

"So how does a man from the great state of Illinois end up as a federal marshal?"

Moriarty shrugged. "I needed a job. I went out west because I'd heard they needed cow hands. My father's a dairy farmer, I grew up working stock. I worked a ranch in New Mexico Territory for a couple of years. When it went bust, I needed work and the marshals were hiring."

"Work didn't agree with you?"

"I was with the marshals for six years. Then I heard of an opening with the railroad, so I applied."

"Been with us ever since?"

"That's right, sir."

"When you were with the marshals did you ever kill a man, Mr. Moriarty?"

Moriarty kept his face impassive. "Yes, sir."

The old man waited. When it was obvious that Moriarty wouldn't volunteer any more information, he went on. "How'd you take to it?"

"It's a filthy business," Moriarty said. "Sometimes, though, the other fella doesn't leave you any choice. I never discharged a weapon that I did not have to."

"Ever shot a man for the railroad?"

"Yes, sir, on two occasions. One man died, one got away."

"Would you say," the old man paused, choosing his words with care, "that you are particularly disconcerted by the presence of the dead?"

"Disconcerted, sir?" Moriarty considered the question. "I don't believe so, no. I've attended funerals. And a few hangings. I didn't faint."

"Mr. Moriarty," the stationmaster said, seeming to come to a decision, "I've got a particularly ticklish piece of work to assign, and I believe that you are the man for the job."

"Thank you, sir," Moriarty said.

"You're familiar with the name Abraham Sutter, I presume?"

"Of course. I'm given to believe he owns a substantial interest in the railroad."

"Used to own," Mr. Cotton corrected. "He died this morning."

Moriarty nodded gravely. "I'd heard that he was ailing."

"A morbid infection of the bowels."

16

There didn't seem to be anything to say to that, so Moriarty just nodded.

"I have been charged with ensuring that Mr. Sutter's will is carried out," Cotton went on. "He has some rather specific instructions regarding the disposition of his remains. He is to be buried in Sacramento, and it was his will that his body be delivered there with all due speed. Overnight, if possible."

Moriarty considered that. "A good train and clear tracks could make that. Will we be leaving soon, sir? I take it that I am to accompany the remains?"

Cotton looked sour. "Mr. Sutter's will also specified certain... *rites* be performed before his body is placed in the casket."

"He was a Latter Day Saint?" Moriarty ventured.

"I would not call him a saint," Cotton opined flatly. "And I believe his wishes regarding his remains are, uh, somewhat in variance to local funerary customs as I understand them. I'll speak frankly, Mr. Moriarty, and trust to your discretion. Abraham Sutter has not been a healthy man for some time, in body or in mind. Quite distressing for those of us who knew him in his younger days. A formidable business intellect at one time, you understand."

Cotton fell silent for a moment, then sighed. "It is my considered opinion that his long history of ill-health adversely effected his brain. Of late he embraced odd ideas. Spiritualism. Theosophy. Oriental superstitions. He became convinced that he could escape the inevitable dissolution of his body—in the flesh, rather than trusting to a spiritual renewal through our Savior."

Moriarty nodded without comment.

"He also came to believe that he was the target of a peculiar secret society, a belief that was almost certainly true in the sense that his wealth was targeted by every charlatan and mountebank this side of the Rockies once it became known he was a devotee of the mystical."

Cotton came to an abrupt halt as if realizing that he had said more than he'd intended. In a more measured tone he added, "Your discretion in these matters is vital."

"Of course, sir," Moriarty said.

"In event, his will specified that he should travel with an escort, and that escort be armed against the possibility that parties would attempt to steal his remains, for... whatever reason," Cotton said. "You will be traveling in his private car, which should by now be hitched to Sacramento Overnight Express."

"The Death Valley Cannonball," Moriarty observed.

Cotton frowned at the nickname. "The Sacramento Overnight Express," Cotton said, emphasizing the company's official name for the run, "is being drawn by the railroad's newest Danforth-Cooke. The engineer and brakeman have been promised a substantial bonus to be in Sacramento by ten tomorrow morning."

Moriarty glanced out the window to the sky. Well after noon, but still some hours until sunset. He considered the route and nodded.

"One mail car, three freight, one passenger, and Mr. Sutter's traveling car. The freight, I understand is mixed sundries, clothing and light goods of that nature. Four or five passengers, I believe. A light train for such a mighty engine. Barring an impediment on the tracks, I anticipate that you will make the deadline handily."

Moriarty stood, feeling that the interview was at its end. Cotton stayed him with an upraised hand.

"Moriarty—that is in Irish name, I believe?"

"It is."

"Are you Catholic?"

"I am."

"I would consider it a great kindness if you would pray for Bram Sutter's soul, while on your journey. He was not a bad man, but I fear towards the end of his life he was... misled."

The intensity .of Cotton's gaze was disconcerting. Moriarty nodded slowly, realized that more was expected of him, and gravely said, "I will pray for Mr. Sutter's soul."

Then he picked up his traveling bag, slung it over his shoulder, and went out into the trainyard.

The engine was a beauty, all right, brand new and gleaming steel. Behind it was the tender, loaded with coal. Even it looked clean and new.

Next was the postal service car, clearly painted as such, the doors secured by ostentatiously large iron padlocks. Behind it was the single passenger car. Moriarty bent and glanced under the car to check the undercarriage and make sure the connections were sound.

When he looked back up, he found himself nearly face to face with a woman in a black dress.

"Excuse me... miss," he said, stammering a bit. At first glance he thought her an old woman, but her face was smooth, girlish. It was only the severity of her gown that gave the impression of age. Her hair was covered by a dark scarf that was pulled back with such precision that it almost seemed a wimple and her vestments a habit. For a moment Moriarty considered amending his greeting to "Sister", so strong was this impression.

Then she smiled at him, and both the appearance of age and ecclesiastic garb faded. She was a lovely girl, too pale and unworn to be a native of the west. From back east, then, or maybe even Europe. Her gown was elegant in its simplicity, unadorned black. A mourner for the late Mr. Sutter, perhaps? Cotton hadn't mentioned any such among the passengers, but perhaps he didn't know.

"Is there a problem with the train?" she asked. Her English was clear, but her very lack of accent suggested that she'd grown up with another tongue.

"No, not at all," Moriarty reassured her quickly. "New engine, new tender. I'm just an old railroad man, checking the cars is second nature."

Her eyes flicked down his suit, registering his lack of uniform. "And what do you do for the railroad, sir?"

"Security, miss," he said automatically.

"I feel safer already," she said. Her smile dazzled him, and while he was dazzled, she turned in a whisper of skirts and was gone into the single passenger car.

Moriarty nodded after her and touched the brim of his hat. He saw several dark figures through the glass, already seated.

A wealthy foreigner, he decided, on a sightseeing trip through the American wilderness. Idly he hoped she had brought her own bodyguards. The Western territories weren't London or Paris, after all.

Then he checked the freight cars, making sure that they were latched.

Then at end, in lieu of a caboose, Mr. Sutter's own car. It was a lavish one, as befitted a part owner of the railroad. Moriarty wasn't impressed, though, he'd seen many such in his time with the company. Under the fine paneling and thick carpet, it was a standard passenger car—a long narrow box with a door at each end and windows along both sides. Much of the original furniture had been removed to make room for a long bier, although the coffin was not yet in evidence. The chairs that remained looked comfortable enough and Moriarty considered that the job, once stripped of its trappings of the macabre, was one of the easiest ones he'd been assigned.

Sit in this fine car and stay awake through the night, watching for boogeymen. He'd been a bodyguard for rich men before, and this time he wouldn't even be expected to make conversation with his charge.

The walls were paneled below the windows, a fine polished rosewood. A moment's investigation revealed that the majority of the panels, when pressed, would open to reveal cabinets of a cunning space-saving design. A pocket library, mostly traveler's tales—the South Seas, Africa, India, the Orient. Interesting. Another panel revealed a small but well-stocked bar. A third held games, chessboard and pieces, a dartboard, several decks of cards and a rack of chips—

The door to the car opened and Moriarty hastily closed the panel and stood. He turned to face the door.

Isaiah Cotton entered and guided four men, who were awkwardly maneuvering an ornate coffin up the steps and through the narrow door. The men wore the uniform of porters and were big men, experienced cargo handlers, no doubt. Still the door was not designed for the task, and it took some sweating and grunting, directed by muttered instructions from Cotton. On the whole the performance had the air of a farce rather the proper solemnity the occasion called for.

In due time the coffin was settled onto the bier, and Cotton dismissed the porters with a curt nod.

"The Sacramento station master will be expecting you," Cotton said, "and it's my understanding that he will handle the paying of the behest."

Moriarty frowned. "Behest?" he asked.

Cotton raised bushy eyebrows in a feigned expression of surprise. "Oh, didn't I mention that? Mr. Sutter's will specifies a payment to his escort. Five hundred dollars, which is certainly a generous sum for one night's work." Cotton's tone made it clear that he felt that was another evidence of the tycoon's mental instability.

"It certainly is," Moriarty agreed, feeling a bit overwhelmed. That was more than he made in a year.

Cotton nodded and turned to leave the car. At the door he paused and said, "You will remember to pray?"

"Yes, sir."

Two minutes later the train was rolling westward along the track.

The setting sun painted the scenery outside the window in fantastic colors, the jagged bones of the Earth sticking out through the skin of the bleeding desert. It seemed impossible that this landscape could belong to the same world as the green hills of Illinois, much less the same country. No matter how long he lived in the West, the high desert never lost its power to astonish him with its savage beauty.

Moriarty turned to look at the coffin. The sides and lid were carved with patterns that struck him as more mathematical that theological, circles with triangles, triangles within circles, lines crossing and re-crossing, but nowhere a human figure or even anything recognizable as script. The pattern was as intricate as a Navajo blanket, and as barren of meaning.

Feeling the weight of his promise to Mr. Cotton upon him, Moriarty retrieved his rosary from his bag and got to his knees, carefully due to the swaying of the train. He lowered his eyes and, beginning with the cross, he murmured, "*Credo in Deum Patrem omnipotentem, Creatorem caeli et terrae...*"

As he prayed, he felt himself relax. He was, his father would have said, an indifferent Catholic. Frequently the railroad had him travel on Sundays, and his address was perpetually "in transit" which precluded any allegiance to a parish. Nonetheless, he did attend mass when he was able, often in tiny Mexican churches where his fair hair and complexion elicited curious looks. He confessed to a priest when time and circumstances allowed. At other times he confessed to the vacant immensity of the night sky, feeling the weight of the heavens upon him, the weight of the glory of God, and cried to the stars, "*Miserere nobis!*"

As he prayed, small bead, large bead, in the old and comforting pattern, he felt the presence of the Holy Family, St. Joseph, the Blessed Virgin, Christ the Redeemer.

Lord, have mercy on me, a sinner.

When he had come to the end of his beads, he made the sign of the cross as he had seen Mexican peasants do it, a touch to forehead, abdomen, each shoulder, then a second pass to make a smaller cross at each spot, then a kiss to the rosary before stowing it carefully back in his bag.

Still on his knees, he addressed himself to the coffin and said, "*Réquiem ætérnam dona ei Dómine; et lux perpétua lúceat ei. Requiéscat in pace. Amen.*"

In English he added, "I did not know this man, but I took his money while he lived, and I owe him my loyalty. I ask that his sins be forgiven in the name of Jesus. *In nómine Patris, et Fílii, et Spíritus Sancti. Amen.*"

If God answered, His answer was inaudible. Moriarty felt, at least, as if he had discharged his promise and his duty in good order. He chose a seat with a good view out the windows and sat back. The key to staying vigilant on a long trip, he'd found, was being comfortable.

The train picked up speed and the miles rolled past.

As the sky grew darker, he lit the lamps that hung in a row down the center of the car. He'd started to wish he'd brought something to eat. There might be some kind of victuals stored in one of the cupboards, but Moriarty didn't much fancy the idea of eating a dead man's food.

In the game cabinet there was a slim volume entitled *101 Diverting Problems In The Game of Chess*. Moriarty took the book, the board, and the pieces. The board, he saw, had a small hole drilled in the center of each square and each piece had a corresponding peg on their base, to prevent the game from upset due to the swaying of the train. He set up the board to match the first puzzle and studied it. He was no master of the game, but it should keep him awake for the hours it would take to reach California.

He'd solved two problems and was studying the third when the train began to slow. He pulled out his watch to check the time and surprised to see how late it had gotten. Time to take on water. He went to the window and saw the lanterns of the engineer and brakeman. They were hurrying to fill the boiler and get moving again, mindful of the bonus Cotton had mentioned.

There was a knock on the door of the car.

It was the forward door and Moriarty hurried to it. The only other railroad employees were at work on the siding, watering the boiler. But why would a passenger be at the door?

It was the woman in black whom he had seen at the Salt Lake Station.

"Miss?" Moriarty asked, confused.

"Heget," she said, stepping past him and into the car. "My name is Heget."

"Miss... Heget," Moriarty said hesitantly, intimidated by her manner, "you should return to your car. We won't be here long, and you won't be able to get back once we start rolling again."

She turned her gaze to him, a soft smile on her lips. "I'll be stuck in here with you? There are worse ways to spend the journey along the twelve hours of the night, I'll wager."

Moriarty frowned and fought to control his anger. There were always some passengers who thought they were above the rules, and it was not uncommon for them to be young, pretty women. No doubt she was accustomed to her smile making men do whatever she wished.

That didn't work on Sean Michael Moriarty.

"Miss Heget," he said sharply. "If you will read your ticket you will see that your passage is subject to conditions set by the railroad and among them is the stricture that you remain in the car to which you have been assigned. Failure to do so can result in your being put off the train."

Her eyes grew wide with an amused surprise. "Why, I do believe that you are serious, Mr. Moriarty. You would leave me in the wasteland to be beset by savages and wild beasts."

"Miss—" Moriarty began.

She held up one hand, graceful and slim, and his voice stilled. She had an imperious manner, one that went beyond that of a simple wealth and privilege. She acted like royalty.

24

"One moment," she said, moving past him to the casket in the middle of the car. "I simply wish to pay my respects."

"You knew Abraham Sutter?" Moriarty asked. He glanced out the window. The lights were still moving around on the siding, evidence that the watering was in progress.

"Intimately," she breathed, gazing down at the patterns carved into the wooden box. "Oh, he was a clever boy, wasn't he?"

Outside the window the lanterns were moving back to the engine.

"Miss, for you own safety—" he began.

She raised her eyes to his. Those eyes were very large and startlingly blue. "We'll talk again," she said, and was gone out the door into the night before Moriarty could react. He went to the door, but her dark clothes made her invisible in the night.

Serves her right if she gets left behind, he thought savagely.

A few minutes later the engine's whistle blew, and the train lurched into motion again.

It was only after he had seated himself and was setting up the chess pieces again that it occurred to him that he had never told her his name. Maybe the engineer had recognized him and mentioned his name to her. Whoever she was it was clear that came from wealth. If she had known Mr. Sutter it was possible—likely, even—that she was related to a shareholder of the railroad.

He sighed. Complications. Freight runs were the best, no one on board save fellow employees, nothing to worry about except track collapses, wild animals, and the occasional bandit gang. He'd take any combination of the three over rich, spoiled passengers any day.

He set up another chess problem and listened to the wheels running over the tracks and the wind rushing past the windows. They were making good time, the engine running smooth and swift as a silver fish cutting through an ocean of night. His eyes felt heavy and he realized all of the sudden that both black bishops were on white squares and he couldn't figure out where he'd made a mistake. He tried to set up the pieces again, but the diagram in the book didn't make any sense. The black queen was threatening the white knight and the black queen looked like Miss Heget, smiling her enigmatic smile. The chessboard wasn't a chessboard anymore, that was the problem. He was trying to set up the pieces on the geometric patterns on the lid of Mr. Sutter's coffin, but that wouldn't work because there were too many pieces all the sudden, dozens of them, pawns and kings and shapes he'd never seen before like twisted tree roots, and all the while the black queen kept laughing at him...

Then the whistle shrieked, and Moriarty's eyes snapped open. The train was stopped. He checked his watch. He'd been dozing over the chessboard while they crossed a hundred miles of desert—

Miss Heget was sitting on a chair across the car, on the other side of the casket from him. Two hulking men, also dressed in black from head to toe, stood behind her chair.

Heart hammering, Moriarty lurched to his feet, upsetting the chair. The three figures across the car reacted no more than a trio of waxworks. The scene was so uncanny that he was sure for a moment that he was still dreaming, and he scrubbed his eyes with his fists and looked again.

The young woman and her two bodyguards were still there, watching him.

Then Heget spoke, "Sit down, Mr. Moriarty. We have business to discuss."

"You're trespassing," Moriarty said, still standing. He felt in his pocket for his revolver. "I am going to have to ask you to leave."

"Please," she spoke with perfect calm, "sit. You have committed a grave injustice. I should like to give you the opportunity to make amends."

"What injustice?" Moriarty backed away clutching his revolver in his jacket pocket. The odds weren't good, with two men in the car who were

26

probably also armed.

"Sit. I will explain."

Moriarty leaned against the window frame. The emergency cord ran along the window frame, inches from his hand. Even if the engineer and brakeman were assisting with the water and coal, they should hear the bell from the engine.

"All that you will accomplish by pulling that," Miss Heget said sharply, "is to get those men killed."

Moriarty was certain that he hadn't even glanced at the cord.

"My other retainers are at the front of the train," the woman continued. "They are constrained at the moment from taking action against mortals who are uninvolved with this affair. If you involve them, they become fair game. My patience is not inexhaustible."

There was no sign from the seated woman, but the two men behind her stepped forward.

Before they could cross the car, Moriarty reached behind him to right the chair he'd knocked over, then sat. "Who are you and what do you want?"

"I told you, I am Heget," the woman said. The two men moved back to stand behind her. Outside the window the train's whistle blew. They'd finished refueling. "And I want what is mine."

Moriarty braced himself as the train lurched into motion again. He noticed that the others didn't yet remained as still as if rooted to the spot. "All right," he said, "What is it that is yours, and how am I keeping you from getting it?"

Heget smiled. "Therein hangs a tale."

She gestured at the window. Moriarty glanced at it, then stared, open-mouthed. Instead of the desert landscape, beyond the window was a swamp, as seen from a boat on a slow-moving river. On the bank of the river was a bonfire, surrounded by figures engaged in some sort of dance.

27

"Natchez," Heget said, "before the war. My... congregation. Young Abraham is there—he's in the owl mask."

Moriarty continued to stare. He could feel the wheels of the train below his feet, rushing through the night, but his eyes told him that they were drifting slowly. He could smell the smoke of the fire, the warm dampness of the mossy air. He heard music, too, a savage rhythm pounded on wooden drums. The figures, he saw, were masked, but wore nothing else except daubs of white mud tracing designs on their bare tanned skin.

"Abraham is thirteen, and he is being consecrated to my service. His mother is officiating the ceremony—she's on the far side of the fire, in the mask with the long horns. See her?"

Moriarty swallowed, his throat dry. He looked back to the woman in the car—if woman she was.

"How?" He couldn't complete the question.

Heget waved that away. "A minor trick. I simply want you to see that I tell you is true."

"*What* are you?"

"That's hardly important," she said. "I am sure that you can form your own opinions on the subject. Suffice to say that I am someone who makes deals and I keep my bargains."

"What kind of deals?"

She seemed exasperated by the question. "The usual kind of deal, Mr. Moriarty. *Everybody* wants *something*. I give it to them."

Another gesture at the window. The scene outside was now a sunlit square in some Eastern town, a large crowd milling around a courthouse. Moriarty was hit with a wave a vertigo because he could still feel the movement of the train, but the window seemed motionless, as if he were standing in a building facing the square.

"In Abraham's case it was wealth," Heget went on. "Are you familiar with the North Georgia Gold Lottery? No? Well, it was in '32, before you were born. After the state removed the Cherokee, they held a drawing to assign mining rights to the land. I arranged for Abraham to win a rich lot, and in very short order his dreams of wealth were realized."

The scene changed again, and Moriarty gripped the windowsill. Whatever magic lantern trick this strange... person was doing, it was giving him vertigo. Now the window seemed to look down over the aisle of a church, as if the train car had been transported to the choir loft.

A wedding was in progress, the pews full of a well-dressed crowd. There were soft murmurs from the bride and groom. Moriarty noticed the church seemed strangely unadorned, lacking even a cross over the altar, and the priest—if priest he was—wore a simple black suit.

"Next he wanted love, and I gave him that, too." Heget went on. "Prudence was such a lovely girl, and from a fine family."

A sigh from Heget. Then, "Sadly, love did not thrive, despite the young couple's advantages. Abraham tired of his bride and sought to replace her with a woman more... in keeping with his tastes. He once again asked for my assistance, and I freely granted it."

The scene outside the window shifted again. It was a bedroom, richly appointed in what was obviously a mansion. A slim woman, moving with the slow, underwater motions of a sleepwalker, crossed the room to a chair. A rope hung from the ceiling beam above the chair. The woman mounted the chair and tied the rope into a crude noose.

Horrified, Moriarty tore his eyes away from the scene. Distantly, he seemed to hear the sound of the chair falling, then the creaking of a laden rope swinging.

"Shall I continue?" Heget asked politely. "For three-score years and ten, as specified by the terms of our contract, I granted him many favors." An earthy chuckle. "Starting with his second wife."

A cry from the window startled Moriarty. It was wild and sensual, a cry of passion. Dark, animal passion. Moriarty refused to turn to look.

Heget gave a wry grin and inclined her head as if conceding the round. Then she continued, "His business thrived. Competitors had unexpected reversals. His own investments blossomed. He always invested in industries on the verge of success. His canny strategies were well known in banking world. People said that Abraham Sutter had 'the touch'. He seemed to know just when a penny could be spent to return a dollar." She paused, ironic eyes above a toothy grin. "As if by magic."

"Through his seventieth year he maintained the physique of a young man." Heget waved a hand airily. "Not too obviously, of course. Nothing that would cause talk. Outwardly he aged just as other men, but he escaped the worse ravages of time. He had none of the annoyances of digestion or joints that bedevil other men of his age. His..." her pause was suggestive "... *vitality* remained undiminished."

She glanced down, smiling sweetly as if indulging a memory both private and sweet. Then she lifted her head to meet Moriarty's eyes.

"At the appointed hour I withdrew my protection, as we had agreed. And even then, I did nothing malicious, nothing to hasten his demise. I simply allowed nature to take its wonted course. It took two years, and he died a wealthy man, pampered by servants and drifting gently away on a warm sea of rum and morphine."

"What does any of this have to do with me?" Moriarty asked coldly.

Heget's eyes flashed with anger. "I am coming to that, young man."

She stood fluidly, moving with an uncanny grace despite the swaying of the rushing train. She crossed to the ornate casket and held her hands above the carved wood, not touching it. "Abraham's lovely mother, Emmalou, was a conjure woman of no small skill. It was she who made the... initial overtures in our relationship. Naturally she passed her knowledge to her son. Later in his life, as he felt his days slipping away, he strove to increase his mastery of the craft. He had the resources to purchase

30

arcane knowledge from the ends of the Earth by that time." A shrug, a gently feminine gesture at odds with what Moriarty had come to know of the other. "Many of my clients do likewise, of course. They search for a way to break our compact before the payment comes due. I indulge such efforts, since they are invariably futile."

Comprehension dawned and Moriarty smiled. "Abraham Sutter found a way."

Heget looked down at the casket. "He found half a way, rather." Then back at Moriarty. "You provided the other half."

"Me?"

"You and..." Heget nearly snarled the words, "the Power you serve."

"The Power," Moriarty said. "You mean—"

"*If you speak that Name in my presence, I will feed your eyes to my ravens,*" Heget's voice boomed through the car and Moriarty flinched back.

The car swayed and he risked a glance out the window. The dessert night, stars swarming above black mountains. Back to his three strange companions. The two men were as still as granite pillars. If he hadn't seen them move earlier, he would suspect they were realistic manikins. Heget was as motionless, leaning over the casket, watching him.

"The Power I serve," he gave her words back to her. "You mean my prayer for Mr. Sutter's soul."

Animation returned to Heget. She nodded. "This construct, crude as it is, will not permit me to directly affect his mortal remains. Ordinarily that would prove only a minor obstacle, but your... *petition* complicates matters."

Moriarty nodded slowly, digesting that. "I see," he said at last.

"And you see why you must rescind your benediction," Heget said firmly.

"What?"

"You have taken what is mine," Heget said, rage showing now in her face

31

and voice, "You and... the Other. Abraham had enough skill as a hedge wizard to build this box for his corpse, but that alone wouldn't have been enough to cheat me of my due. He couldn't not petition for assistance from the Other on his own behalf, not after he had signed the compact with me. Only one who had shared the Feast of the Lamb could make invoke that protection."

"And now you expect me to..." Moriarty struggled for words. "To... what? Pray for his damnation?"

"Nothing so melodramatic!" Heget laughed. "Simply speaking aloud, the intention will be enough."

"I... can't do that."

"Of course, you can! It doesn't even have to be in Latin—you must know the language doesn't matter, it's just a silly affectation. Just admit that you were wrong to intercede on Abraham's behalf."

Moriarty shook his head. "But I wasn't wrong."

Heget laughed. "Not wrong? Praying for the soul of a black magician? If you had known what manner of man he was, would you have asked for his salvation?"

Moriarty considered that for a long moment, feeling the click of the rails under his feet. "Maybe not," he admitted. "But that doesn't mean I was wrong to... do what I did. It's not for me to decide who is worthy of salvation."

"But that is what you did," Heget said. "You took it upon yourself to intercede for Abraham."

"I made the petition," Moriarty replied. "I didn't grant it."

"*You had no right to make that petition!*"

Moriarty nodded. "No right at all," he agreed sadly. "It's not by right that we approach... that One."

"Abraham is *mine*," Heget snarled. "He gave himself to me, freely, and I paid him all that I promised him and more. Justice demands that I get what is mine."

"Grace demands that you do not."

"You serve a cheat and a liar," Heget said. "A thief. That power turned against us—we who were once his most favored children. Do you think that you will receive better?"

"I can't say. I know I don't deserve better."

A sharp bark of laughter. "No, you don't, Sean Michael Moriarty. I can see your soul and it is a small and ugly thing. You live your entire life from bloody birth to bloody death in the time it takes me to draw a breath. You have murdered. You have lain with whores. You have stolen—stolen from your own father. Your heart is as black as mine and your crimes are less only because you are so weak."

Moriarty was silent.

"You think that you will be welcomed? What makes you think that? Why should some piece of meat like be admitted into that eternal kingdom when I—I who was born there, who walked those fields in ages past—am cast out?"

"Because I asked for forgiveness."

Heget screamed with rage then and threw herself at Moriarty and for a moment all that he could see was her onrushing face, distorted into a thing of horror by blind imbecilic hate. In terror he threw himself backwards and tumbled onto the floor of the car, her scream going on and on—

—and becoming the scream of the train whistle.

He was lying on the floor of the traveling car, the overturned chair beside him. The car was slowing. He lifted his head.

He was alone in the car, except for the oddly carved casket. To the east, the sky glowed red.

He got up and went to the window. Painted on the side of the water tank was *Roseville, California.*

"I slept the whole night away," Moriarty said softly to himself.

It was dawn.

When the train stopped, he got out onto the platform, stretching his stiff limbs. The engineer and brakeman were filling the boiler, the steam adding to the already considerable heat.

"How are we doing?" Moriarty asked.

"Great," the engineer said. "We'll have breakfast in Sacramento."

"How are the passengers?"

"Passengers?" the brakeman asked.

Moriarty turned to gesture at the car, then froze in place. There was no passenger car. The engine, a mail car, three freight cars, and then Abraham Sutter's traveling car. That was all.

"Didn't we..." Moriarty was suddenly sure of the answer, but asked it anyway, "have a passenger car when we left Salt Lake? Did we drop it somewhere along the way?"

The engineer and brakeman exchanged a look. The engineer answered. "Not this run. Heck, you know the Death Valley Cannonball is a mail run. We almost never have passengers."

"I must have been confused," Moriarty said.

"Must have been," the brakeman agreed. "They got some coffee boiling in the station office. Why don't you grab yourself a cup?"

"I think I'll do that."

When the train got back underway Moriarty collected the scattered chess pieces and board and set up another problem, but he found it hard to concentrate. Instead he looked out the window at desert landscape, growing bright in the clean light of the morning sun. What a dream he'd had.

He looked back at the coffin containing Abraham Sutter's mortal remains.

"As I am," he said softly, "you once were. As you are, I must someday be."

34

He looked back at the chessboard. *White knight takes black queen,* he thought.

Mate.

Misha Burnett has little formal education, but has been writing poetry and fiction for around forty years. During this time he has supported himself and his family with a variety of jobs, including locksmith, cab driver, and building maintenance.

His first four novels, *Catskinner's Book*, *Cannibal Hearts*, *The Worms Of Heaven*, and *Gingerbread Wolves* comprise a series, collectively known as *The Book Of Lost Doors*.

Major influences include Tim Powers, Samuel Delany, William Burroughs, and Phillip K. Dick.

More information about upcoming projects can be found at http://mishaburnett.wordpress.com

Llano Estacado

Jackson Kuhl

Tom Tucker went up to Santa Fe to confirm title to his land. It took him three-and-a-half days to ride there and another two waiting for the clerk to see him.

"I'm sorry, señor," said the clerk, sliding the paperwork across the desk. "The parcel has already been given to someone else."

"What?" said Tucker. "I've lived and ranched that land almost ten years. My grant's right here." He tapped the paper on the desk. "It's all legal."

The clerk pushed into the red leather of his armchair and gazed at Tucker over the rims of his Ben Franklin glasses. "Your land was granted by the Texians. They had no right to do so. The Mexican government does not recognize the authority of a breakaway *departamento*."

"Texas is part of the U.S. now. You recognize the legitimacy of the United States, don't you? You recognize the papers they write?" Tucker and his wife had run from Kentucky, four months behind on the rent, six months on their store tab, hounded by a collector all the way to the state line. The note pinned to the door of their shack is what alerted their creditors. *GTT,* it said— *Gone To Texas.* There in Texas they homesteaded a free parcel, way to the west on the llano. A new life, a clean slate. Before the war.

The clerk shrugged. "*Nuevo México* is Mexico. Not <u>Tejas</u>. Not *Estados Unidos*."

"And I respect the authority of Mexico. I'm a Mexican citizen now." Tucker reached inside his jacket, felt around. Thought a moment. Made a decision. He pulled a dozen bills from the pocket and plopped them in front of the clerk. It was all the cash he had. It would be a hungry three-and-a-half days back.

"I was remiss in paying the filing fee," he said low.

The clerk shook his head at the worn banknotes. "My filing fee is much more than that, señor. Much more." He adjusted his spectacles, fussed with books and papers on his desk. "Go home, señor."

The new landowner was Capitan Baltasar Batalla Farias.

"I own all this, everything you see," he told Tucker and his wife as they stood on their porch. Batalla and his men didn't even bother to dismount. "You think you owned this land, but you never did. You can stay in the house. Only now you must pay rent to me."

"You son of a bitch—we *built* this house," said Tucker's wife. Her name was Clover.

Batalla and his men laughed. "Do not worry, señora. I would be a fool to come from Mexico City and ignore someone like your husband. Doubtless he knows this land better than anyone. Every playa lake, every blade of grass." He addressed Tucker: "You can work for me. I will make you chief of my *vaqueros*."

Tucker considered the arithmetic. If not, they would have to sell their cattle piecemeal to pay rent. And Tucker and his wife, out there alone, barely made enough as it was to buy the things they couldn't grow or make.

"I'll take the job," he told Batalla.

"You should kill him," Clover said that night, lying next to Tucker.

38

"Goddamn son of a bitch. Plug him square above the nose."

"What good would that do?" he asked. "Then the Mexican government would arrest me as a murderer. I want them to recognize my claim, not lock me up." He didn't think less of his wife for saying her mind. Tucker believed women were more inclined to violence than men, deep down. He had heard stories about when Apache captured prisoners, it was the squaws who did most of the torture.

"Cut his damn balls off."

"I can't very well break the same law I want supporting me," he said.

So, Tucker became Batalla's foreman. Over the next five months Batalla ordered a big house built, along with stables and outbuildings and a bunkhouse for the hands. Batalla bought two-hundred head of cattle, and Tucker and his men had plenty of work branding and herding and driving.

"This is the birth," said Batalla to Tucker. They stood in the purple light of evening looking at the almost-completed house, wrapped in scaffolds. Beyond was nothing but flatness and grass except to the far, far west. "Of my *hacienda*, my estate. The beginning of a long dynasty."

"Sure thing, Don," said Tucker.

Batalla pointed with his cigar. "You *Americanos* fought hard for this land. I can understand why."

"Land gives food. Gives water. A landowner has a better sense of what's coming the next day. It's worth fighting and killing for."

Batalla sucked deeply, blew smoke. "Tomorrow I will send for my children in Mexico City. It is time they came home."

Don Batalla had two children. The son, Marcos, was thirteen.

"Did you really fight in the war?" he asked Tucker one day.

Tucker was waiting in the yard to see his *patrón*. Marcos, playing there, had suddenly noticed him. He looked up at Tucker, head cocked to the side, shielding his eyes from the sun. The daughter, near marrying age, sat on the porch doing needlework.

"I did," said Tucker with satisfaction. "I served as a volunteer, 9th Company, under Mirabeau Lamar. I was at Monterrey. I was with old Zack Taylor when he surrendered to Santa Anna at Buena Vista."

Marcos burst out laughing. "Ha ha, you fucking gringo!" he said. "Santa Anna gave all this land to my papa as a reward for his bravery in the war. Because you *Americanos* are too chickenshit to fight!"

"Marcos, go inside," said his sister.

"You fucking yellow coward. Ha ha!"

"Marcos!"

The boy obeyed, still chortling.

"Who taught him English?" said Tucker to the girl. "I think he's got the hang of it."

"He's a little brat," she said. But she smiled at her needlework because the boy hadn't said anything she disagreed with.

This was Batalla's dynasty. His estate. The inheritors of his *hacienda*.

So next day, Tom Tucker rode off to become an outlaw. And Clover Tucker, standing on their front porch with hands on her hips, thought how strange a man was: like a mule, shouldering a great burden without so much as a complaint but a horsefly, pricking his neck, will drive him to fury.

There were other displaced landowners, other Tom Tuckers, and by ones and twos they came together. They wandered the plains and occasionally came through and tore up the saloons of a town. They camped in the canyons and gullies beyond the ridge, hide-outs, because there were other Batallas too, *hacendados* come north, to settle land—to hold the frontier by possession. After the war, Santa Anna figured he didn't need the headache of a seditious state, so he let Washington keep Texas, although it was a smaller reduced Texas than what the Anglos had intended. A string of Mexican settlements soon germinated along the border between *Nuevo México* and the States, Santa Anna just doing what the Romans had done in

Britain and Germany to prevent any more squatters or land-jobbers drifting in like snowflakes through an open window.

But those Tom Tuckers, most of them veterans of the war between the US and Mexico, loved nothing better than raiding and burning the *casas* of the Batallas.

They would sweep across the grassland at sunset and back again toward the western bluffs at night's end. At the start, it was spite that fueled Tucker's people. A moonless night, no breeze, the crickets chirping and the cicadas rattling; then a growing rumble of hoof beats, the earth like the skin of a drum. Through the gates they thundered, the ranch hands running from their bunks with repeaters and revolvers to be shot dead in their drawers. Lanterns lit and thrown into the hay of the barn, glass smashed, the house breached. They killed and they stole money and liquor and they broke china and furniture and if the *hacendados* were smart, then they and their families were running out the back door as the raiders came in the front. The band hated the Mexicans, but they hated their estates more—it was the *buildings* and *things* they hated.

A party of hacendados came to Batalla.

"Give us his woman," they demanded. "We know her husband is their leader. We will hold her until he stops, and if he doesn't, we will kill her."

Batalla scoffed. "I would sooner give you my own daughter. If any harm should come to the *señora*, Tucker will blame me. Then my own *hacienda* will be forfeit."

"It isn't fair your home should be safe while ours burn," they said.

"Then you should fight better," said Batalla.

"We should raid Batalla," said Goose Engel one evening. A steader, like Tucker, who had owned a ranch taken from him.

Everybody looked at Tucker. "Plenty of softer targets," he said.

"Why not?" said Engel. "Friend of yours?" Daring him.

"You know why. My wife is still a tenant of his."

Engel snapped a stick, threw the halves into the fire. "We all have family, Tucker. We all run risks. And they know it, too."

Tucker surveyed the faces in the firelight. To play favorites with the *hacendados* was a sure way to turn them against him. Fair was fair.

Afterwards Batalla went to the cabin, kicked in the door. Wet, stinking of smoke, smeared with ash. He battered Clover to the floor.

As he stood over her, he reached to undo his belt.

"You think this is bad now," she told him through a split lip, "Then keep going. He'll show you bad."

Batalla stopped. Breathed. Stuck a finger under her bleeding nose.

"You tell him: never again."

Capitan Batalla complained to Santa Fe. When they did nothing, he and a committee rode down to Mexico City to lobby in person. Were they not loyal, tax-paying citizens of *México*? Send the army north and rid them of this pestilence! The bureaucrats shrugged; they had no time for bandits—there were Indians or insurrectionists who needed killing elsewhere. But Batalla was a decorated hero, a military man. They gave him powder and shot and a field piece stripped from some old fort. Sent them on their way. *Buena suerte, señores.*

Batalla and the rest returned north and mustered a posse. Began chasing Tucker and his band back and forth across the grassland, their cannon bouncing in its carriage behind them. The outlaws traveled lighter, moved faster. But it wore them down. Kept them too busy to do anything else. Food ran low.

"We should divvy up," Tucker told his men. "Like cattle in a thunderstorm. They can't rope all of us. Then we'll meet again in a few months."

"You think they'll do the same?" said Goose Engel. "They will not. They'll keep together. Come after a single group in a big bunch."

Tucker nodded. "You're probably right. Though the rest will get away."

"Meaning you?"

"Meaning just what I said." Tucker tightened a saddle strap, not looking at Engel. Kept his voice level and severe. He had never aspired to the role—just a bunch of *hombres locos* following another *hombre loco* because he made the most sense. And yet as a boy in Kentucky he had learned it was much easier climbing up a tree than climbing back down. "Some will get away. Batalla will follow the others."

"I know what group you'll be in," said Engel.

"So do I."

Thinking it in his head, Tucker hadn't been sure which way Batalla would go. But after that Tucker made damn sure the posse chased him and a few volunteers while Engel and the rest rode off free.

They staked a camp at the edge of the Mescalero, their backs to the canyon below, and lit their cook fires so Batalla couldn't help but come after.

"Surrender, Señor Tucker!" Batalla called from the trailhead leading into the camp. It was a bottleneck—the only exit. "Come out and I will hang you quick. No abuse, I promise. No pain."

Tucker yelled from behind the hasty earthworks of dirt and juniper they had constructed. "I thank you, Don, but I can't do it!"

Batalla called again. "Your wife—Señora Tucker. Without her man, she must work for me now. She works in my *cocina*."

"She's a good cook."

"I would not know. She does not cook. I have her fetch the well water, milk the cows. The most menial of tasks. She is a proud and strong woman. Reduced to a kitchen maid because you abandoned her."

"Her and me never agreed on politics."

Batalla tried another tack. "This cannon is very deadly, señor. You and I have both seen war. Seen what it can do. Men, their arms and legs blown

43

off. Their flesh torn. Their bones shattered. Very agonizing. I urge you to reconsider."

No answer was forthcoming.

A terrible siege started. Batalla's men were happy Tucker didn't surrender; it had been a great bother dragging the six-pounder and its shot all this way. Now they could finally use it. Pack the powder and ball, stand back and put the fire to the hole. Big fireworks.

The posse smashed the earthworks to hell and blew the rock apart until chips of stone rained down and bit their skin. The defenders shot back with pistols and carbines, to little effect. The cannon roared like an angel's trumpet.

Finally, Batalla ordered them to stop. Listened. Silence. Were the outlaws dead? Where were the screams of the wounded?

Carefully, guns drawn, Batalla and his men tiptoed through the cratered wreckage of the camp. Slipped through the holes in the earthworks. Expecting maimed bodies, bloody appendages.

Nothing. Nobody. Instead, a spar of wood thrust into the ground, a pulley at its end. Lines and ropes weaved into a sling to lower their horses, one by one. Below, in the canyon, Tucker and his volunteers, on horseback, picked their way downslope to the river. The earthworks were a shield to obscure the action, the cannonry a perfect blanket over the whinnying and terror of the suspended horses.

Batalla slammed his hat on the ground, stamped his heels into the dust.

A frostbit winter swept in. The posse disbanded. Batalla sat in his study— his rebuilt study—and wrote letters to Mexico City. The replies he crumpled and hurled into the fire. A tall glass of Madeira swirled in hand while he composed. Then, in a heat, his pen scratched off fresh epistles.

Tucker and his men endured. Outside. In rain and cold. Through sickness. Whittling away, leaving them hairy and lean.

Some nights Tucker would sneak home. Hide his horse in the barn, be up and out before dawn.

"The daughter's in charge of the kitchen," said Clover. "She lords it over me. *My papa owns you, my papa owns everything and everybody.* Curses me but knows better not to hit."

It was hard doing what she did, sure. Hard work. In the daytime with *them.* In the evenings, the countless repairs and chores the house required, the meals she had to cook for herself. Never-ending nights.

But Tucker had no idea how to get out.

"I've made a mess of things," he said.

"Their mother died years ago."

"I keep thinking how I could've done it different. Maybe just quit and moved to town. Opened a store."

"With what money? We could've sold if we had anything to sell besides the heifers. Cowboy, we don't even own this house."

He rolled over to look at her, at the profile of her face in the lamplight. He ran his thumb along the creases at the corners of her mouth. They were new, since coming to the *llano.* But when had they first appeared? He couldn't say.

"The kid Marcos says he knows why we never had children," she told him. "Says your cock's too soft."

They both laughed.

"I hate that little shit," she said.

In the spring, Tucker and his people met up with Engel. There were men with Engel that Tucker didn't recognize. Not angry steaders, normal folk, turned to raiding because of injustice but men with stares that challenged you to say something. A few other men, good men who had ridden with Tucker before but had gone off with Engel, were absent.

It went okay at first. Tucker's men had to retell their escape from the Mescalero Ridge a few times. Engel nodded and smiled, agreeing it was clever. Where had Engel and his people spent the winter? Engel nodded and chuckled some more.

He suggested they celebrate their reunion by robbing the bank at Knowles.

"Now hold on," said Tucker. "Those are our people. Not *hacendados*. Bank tellers, shopkeepers. They're just regular folk putting their silver in that bank."

Engel shrugged. "It's no difference to me. Why should they have money when I lost my land? They should tithe some in the basket."

"That's not how we work."

"It is now. We're going after that bank."

Tucker forced himself to relax. His hands near his belt. "We're not criminals. We're going to start up again, attacking the *haciendas*." Steer it toward the issues, about what could happen if they went the other way. Reason with him, let Engel think he came to the right opinion on his own. "We do this until the Mexican government gives us our property back. We start robbing banks—they ain't never gonna give us anything."

Engel looked around at his new friends. "My associates and I think different. Face it, old man. Our land is gone. There's only money now. Only survival."

Engel pulled his six-gun.

Tucker stepped close, chopped at the forearm. The gun spilled away. Engel slapped at his right hip with his free hand and a knife arced at Tucker.

Risley, who had been with him at Mescalero, tossed Tucker a Bowie.

They circled, chests pounding, breathing hard, swiping and slashing and stabbing. Then closing. A block with the wrist. A kick to a knee. Tucker grabbed hold of Engel's knife hand while keeping his free to cut. Crossed behind the ankle, tripped him.

Engel lay flat on the ground, Tucker's knife poised over his heart. Tucker heaved as if he had sprinted a mile in his boots, the laceration across his chest seeping. Another scar to add to the exhaustion and the arthritis and the lumbar pain.

"Take him," Tucker said to the men he didn't know, the rough men. "Take your boy and get out of here. Don't ever cross me again."

That evening Clover Tucker heard hooves, footsteps, hard knocking. She dried her hands on her apron and removed the Winchester from over the door. She lifted the bar.

Capitan Batalla pushed aside the rifle and strode into the room. "Is he here?"

"Who?" she asked. "My husband?"

"I know he comes here," said Batalla, "To see you."

Clover said nothing, held the rifle in the crook of her arm.

Batalla sat at the table where she chopped food and ate her supper, crossed his boots on its boards. "I'm glad you see him," he said, smiling. "I need you to give him a message next time."

"You don't have to threaten me. He won't do it again," she said.

"It's not that," said Batalla. "The other *hacendados* and I—we have had enough."

"Enough?" She didn't know what to think. "You're leaving?"

Batalla burst out laughing. "No, no. You misunderstand. We've had enough of *Mexico*." He poured a splash of whiskey into a cup. Needle and thread lay beside it on the table, alone and apart from any needlework or darned socks. "We are tired of how the national government ignores us. We send them taxes. In return we get *nada*. In a way your husband showed this to us." He drank the whiskey. "*Nuevo México* is soon to decide it will no longer be part of the *república*."

"*Nuevo México* decides?" asked Clover. "Or you and the *hacendados*?"

"They are the same."

"And what do you want with my husband?"

"We will need an army. Fighting men—every man we can get. To go against the national government when they come north. When they *finally* come north. In return, we will grant your husband's people amnesty and plots of land for their own. Not as much as they had before the war, perhaps. But enough."

Clover said, "Even if I tell him this, how will his men know it's not an ambush? A way to flush them out and shoot them."

Batalla chuckled again. Shrugged. "I am too tired of chasing your husband across the plains. Do you know how much it vexes my soul that they evade me in a country so *flat*?"

When she had barred the door after Batalla, Clover said, "I think he may be telling the truth."

Tom Tucker walked out from the dark bedroom where he had listened to the conversation. He laid his Colt on the table, poured a slug of whiskey into the cup. Knocked it back. His shirt was open, the line across his ribs throbbing where his wife had stitched him shut. "He's a lying sack."

"Tom," she said, "This could be it. What we've both been suffering for."

"More like it's a trick as you smelled."

"You could arrange a meeting. Somewhere safe, out on the prairie. Six of his men, six of yours. If he hands you the deeds, you enlist."

"What good are papers from *him*? We'd still have to win the damn war for them to be worth anything."

"It's better than what Mexico's offering."

"What's to say he won't back out, even if we do win? Him and his buddies will be the new law. Nothing to make them keep their word."

"He won't do that," said Clover. "That time—when you burned the *hacienda*. He was so angry." She folded her arms. "He's afraid of you. Knew he had to punish me just enough to keep you from coming around again. He knows if he crosses you, you'll come after him personal."

"I thought you wanted me to shoot him."

"I'd rather have our land back."

Tucker stared into the empty whiskey jug. Went over to the counter, knelt, hooked aside the curtain. Nothing but bottles of lye in the cupboard.

"Do you have to go tonight?" she asked.

"No."

She had hoped he would say that.

Supplies were low, the men antsy. They needed to hit a *hacienda*. But Tucker thought long and hard about what Clover had said. *He's afraid of you.* This whole time, believing he's a bedbug going up against a giant. But maybe he did have some capital after all. Not property, not money, but something.

And yet—if they raided a hacienda now, it might sour the deal, harden the *hacendados* against them. Or it could make Batalla more impatient to bargain.

Even if Tucker and Batalla spit on their palms and shook hands, payment still assumed success over Mexico. Against an army that had beaten the Americans, who had beaten the British. When Batalla couldn't whip a pack of starved dogs living under his own nose.

Tucker's indecision chose for him. Risley and a few others went into town to spend their last money on frijoles and cornmeal. They couldn't afford bacon, at least not without pointing guns. Came back quiet, faces cold. Tucker knew something had happened. It came out after dinner, once the coffee had been poured.

"Saw your woman today," Risley said to him, "Coming out of the store."

"Is that right?" It was strange Clover would go there. Knowles was closer.

"The boys and me went into the Dorado for a splash," Risley said. "Heard some news. Turns out your old friend Don Batalla has gone sesesh. Offering pardons and land to anyone who joins up."

Tucker could feel all eyes on him. He kept his gaze in the fire.

"Did you know about this?"

49

"I did," said Tucker.

"And you didn't feel right to share it?"

"I believe it's salt in a snare."

"There's a deadline," said Risley. "You have to go in before sundown tomorrow or no dice. Then you stay outlaw permanent. You were going to let that pass without telling us."

Tucker shook his head. "I had not heard that part before."

"We should trust you?"

"Yes."

Risley sipped his coffee. "I'll never forget that day on the Mescalero. But I'm tired of beans."

They left the next morning.

"I'll join the Mexicans when they come north," Tucker told Clover. "The army will need scouts. I can tell them anything they want, take them any place they want to go. And when it's done, I'll demand the land."

His wife, sitting across from, poured whiskey into the chipped coffee cup. Swirled it.

"Hell, they gave it to Batalla after they beat us. He'll be gone. Shot or hanged. Why wouldn't they turn it over to me as payment?"

She poured the lightning down her long throat. Her eyes watered. "You won't take a deal from someone we know but you believe in a dream from somebody you don't?"

Tucker smacked the table. "I'll join the Mexican army," he said. "This is it. Our chance. What we've been fighting for."

Clover stared over his shoulder, dreamy. She almost never drank. "I wish I had been able to give you a baby. With a baby, you never would've run off."

"I didn't run off. I went to war."

"What would it have been like, you think? With babies."

Tucker wondered what had gotten into her. "I suppose it would depend if we had boys or girls. A boy could've been the man of the house. Worked himself so you could work less."

"A mother always works more no matter what chores the children do."

"You wish I'd never gone out on the *llano*," said Tucker.

"I wish it had gone otherwise. I just —" She put her hand on his, lying on the tabletop. "I think about, sometimes, that other woman. Looking into the glass and seeing a woman tired from feeding and cleaning babies all day. Seeing that woman go gray and wrinkly. Seeing the man going gray beside her."

"The house is too small."

"You were going to build a room for them."

"Would have, too," he said. "This wasn't supposed to happen. It's been one thing after another, ever since Batalla. Losing to the Mexicans just ate up the seasons."

"Knowing you," she said a little too loud, "by the time the room was done, the children would've already moved out and the house would be the perfect size for us again."

"We can still have that." He stabbed a finger at his chest. "It's because of *me* the Mexican army is coming north."

"We'll never have that. I can't make babies."

He squeezed her palm. "Did I ever once complain about it?"

She was too drunk to do anything that night except sleep. Next morning, he rode south to meet the Mexican army. They dragged their heels but come north they did. They couldn't afford to have *another* Texas on their borders.

It was a short campaign. The Texians tossed some guns and powder across the border but the supplies Batalla hoped would come from Washington never arrived—their noses were too deep in the slave issue to look much at anything else. Tucker heard Risley was made captain before being crushed by a falling horse at Portales. Goose Engel and his men were rounded up and shot.

Batalla they kept locked up in the Santa Fe courthouse during the trial. They told Tucker he had asked for him. They let Tucker into the cell and he sat on the wooden stool.

"Tom," Batalla said. "Thank God you're here." His face was drawn, sick. His collar open, no hat on his head.

"I would've come anyway," said Tucker, "because we need to talk."

"Yes."

"What did you do to her?"

"To her?" Batalla's eyes bugged. "To her? What did I do to *her*?"

Tucker had been back to the house only once, when the army was close to Batalla's land. The door latched. Inside dead greenbottles on the sills. Mice in the pantry. A note on the table. "Why did you run her off? I thought you were better than that."

"I didn't run her off. She ran away. On his fifteenth birthday." Batalla's voice choked, almost a sob. "For Marcos."

"The boy?" Tucker asked. "I don't understand."

"My daughter wouldn't let her cook," he said. "Just pump water and milk the cows. So, your wife put it in the milk for the cake. The doctor said his insides melted like lard in a pan."

Tom Tucker looked at him.

"I went around, after. To the shopkeepers. She had been in their stores. Every few months. Knowles once, Pearl another time. Never the same place twice so nobody caught on. Rat poison. Or lye."

The weight of it bore down upon him, a landslide. What Tucker had done. The whole time he believed all the risk was his, running crazy on the plains. She was safe, under the nose of the enemy. But he had left her alone. Alone with nothing but that anger.

Lord in Heaven forgive me for my stupidity.

"I realized later I had paid for it. The poison. The *tlacos* I had given her for her work. Where else could she have gotten the money? You?" Batalla laughed.

Tucker said, "I'm sorry to hear about your boy." And he was. "But listen. The more I stew on it, the more I know I'm to blame for her going away. She stopped believing in me. With good reason. So, whatever happened to you and me, it's our own fault."

"*How dare you?*" Batalla lunged forward. "There are only two people to blame, and one of them is sitting here now." He reached into his waistband, pulled a Derringer the damn fool guards had missed.

Tucker spilled sideways off the stool, but it was no use. Not at that range.

They fished around in his gut but never discovered the .40-caliber round. They stitched up the mess and left Tucker prone in bed, immobilized by agony, as the sepsis crept in. Batalla, they hanged.

As Tucker lay there, unable to sit up or even roll over, he gripped tight the note he found in the house, afraid some nurse or doctor would steal it when he was asleep or distracted. He would study her handwriting, read it again. Wonder how she made out. She must have had it fixed in her mind that last night, set upon what she was going to do. She hadn't told him. He wished he could have seen her again instead of Batalla. She had been abandoned for that land, beaten for it. And she still didn't have it. She didn't have babies. Didn't even have a husband most times.

Those three letters the only record of her he had left. *GTT,* they said.

Jackson Kuhl's fiction has been published most recently in *Nightscript*, *Weirdbook*, the latest volume of the *Horror Library* series, and *Black Static*. He is also the author of the weird-Western collection, *The Dead Ride Fast*, and the biography, *Samuel Smedley, Connecticut* Privateer.

DUSK WOMAN

J. CONRAD MATTHEWS

The wind howled along the plateau. Snow had fallen the night before and the wind cut through Nathaniel Lee's driving gloves like knives. It drove tiny specks of ice into his face where it swirled looking for a way past his muffler and into his jacket.

The air was thin and colder for that than Nathaniel had hoped but not planned for. He was a skilled smith, farrier, and cartwright and planned on making good money off the miners in the boomtowns to the north of Cottonwood. He had brought plenty of food, blankets, and other goods. But he had been alone on the trail except for wolf tracks several hours old. It looked like they had been ranging the area sometime before midnight. The edges of the tracks were windblown, and they had frozen hard with the morning snap.

The horses did not like breaking trail through the snow any more than Nathan liked driving in it. Nick, his cattle dog sat inside the covered wagon out of the wind and snow like any sensible being, but he did not rest easy. The big black dog gave a low rumbling growl.

"I know they're out there," Nathan said in a soothing voice, "They show themselves, we'll do something about it."

Nathan was driving a Studebaker covered wagon, he hoped the wind would not tear off the canvas, although it was mild by the standards of Idaho territory. When he left Boise, the weather was clear and sunny although not exactly balmy. Up here on the plateau it decided winter deserved another go.

Nathaniel was a big man with thick callused hands from working hot metal. His heavy limbs and broad chest said that Nathaniel Lee was not a stranger to hard work.

A Greener shotgun rested across his legs muzzle to his left and he had a pair of Colt Navy conversions rested in holsters at his right hip and a belly draw on his left hip. Lee had picked them up in the war and had them converted to cartridge firing .38 caliber weapons.

A rabbit broke cover to his right from behind a clump of sage brush about twenty yards out. Nick 'whuffed' out a breath and gave a small whine. *Getting closer, damn it!* Nathaniel thought.

An old Indian man dressed in tattered layers of blankets and castoffs stepped out on the trail ahead of Nathaniel. Nathaniel could see a small bundle of rags that was a child of indeterminate sex huddled at the edge of the trail. He would not have sworn it was living save for seeing the breath.

"Whoa," Nathaniel said to the horses he stopped the wagon and set the brake.

"What can I do for you? Do you speak English?"

The old man shook his head, but the bundle of rags spoke up revealing it was a young girl, "No, grandfather cannot speak English, but I do my father was a white man." The girl stood, and Nathaniel could see under the hunger and privation that her complexion was a bit lighter than his own weathered face and hands. Certainly, much lighter than the old man who was burned nearly black as a piece of old jerky.

The old man spoke a language full of sibilant sounds or perhaps it was because he was missing teeth, "Grandfather would like to know if we can trade for food."

Nick growled from inside the wagon.

"Sure, we can talk, but you best tell whomever is sneaking up on the back of my wagon to come out in the open where we can talk civil-like, or ol' Nick will bring 'em out right-quick."

Nathaniel's voice was polite, but he was serious, Nick brooked no fooling around with Nathaniel's property.

The girl looked frightened and said something quick and low to 'Grandfather' who answered her in voice full of hopelessness and fatigue, "That is my older sister. Grandfather did not want her to come out in case you were like other white men."

"I'm like myself, Miss," Nathaniel replied, "Tell your sister to swing wide around the wagon and join you and your grandfather. Then we can palaver."

Nick kept up his low rumble but did not bark or give other alarm, he was just warning the person not to get close to 'the boss" wagon.

A young woman joined the two, there was a distinct resemblance to both, more than just being in the same tribe or band would bring.

"Alright, now that we're here why don't we get acquainted? I'm Nathaniel Lee, my buddy in the wagon is Nick, he's a bit womanish and avoids the snow when he can."

"I'm Mary and my sister is Victoria, named for the queen," Mary said, "White men call grandfather Red Wolf."

"Very pleased to meet you," Nathaniel said giving a genuine smile, "Does your sister speak English or are you the chief negotiator for this rendezvous?"

Red wolf smiled at 'rendezvous', undoubtedly he had been to one or heard of them. The last rendezvous had ended years before.

"I speak English," Victoria answered, "We had the same father, Ian MacDougal, he taught us English and Scottish and French."

"We'll that's a sight more than I can claim," Nathaniel laughed.

"What do you want to trade for?"

"Food," Mary said promptly, "We need food."

Victoria said something in their native tongue, Nathaniel had a fair idea of what she was saying even without knowing the words.

"It's alright," Nathaniel said, "I do have food to trade. Do you have horses?"

"Yes," Mary said at the same time Victoria said, "No."

"Well those, yes-no horses will be hungry too, I guess. Let's have a look-see at what we have in the back."

Nathaniel opened the back of his wagon and Nick jumped out he trotted over to sniff the girls and the old man, gave a 'whuff' and trotted back to Nathaniel's side.

"What can you carry?" Nathaniel said.

The three spoke together and after a moment and Mary said, "We have two horses, but they are thin, we will pack what we can if you are willing to sell."

"Hmm, I don't see what you have to trade."

"We have a blanket," Victoria said suddenly and hurried into the brush. She came back out with a thick woolen blanket somebody had woven by hand.

"That looks fine, let's see if I have anything to match that," Nathaniel said.

He rummaged around in the wagon and started stacking goods on the end of the wagon. "I have an extra bushel of dried fruit, apples, apricots, raisins, and pears. Hmm, a few cans of tinned meat, some canned vegetables, let me see here, yup some cheese." Nathaniel kept stacking food. He had quite a bit of food. He had stocked up and had plenty to spare. If he had to tighten his belt before he got to Cottonwood, so be it.

"The blanket is not worth—" Victoria began.

"No, no you are right Miss, right as rain," Nathaniel said, "I'll throw in some of my old blankets." Nathaniel put some thick woolen blankets on the stack.

"That is too much," Victoria said firmly, but her eyes roved over the stack of cans and sacks.

A horse whickered from at least a mile back and Nick growled.

The girls looked panicked and Red Wolf looked resigned.

"I take it you don't want to meet the men coming?"

"No!" Mary said, "They will put us in the stockade and say we stole grandfather's blanket."

"Ah, well we can't have that, bring your horses and tie them to the back of my wagon."

"Mister Red Wolf if you would be so kind as to get into the wagon and stay quiet," Nathaniel offered a step with his own hands and helped the old man into the back. Victoria came out of the bushes with two of the scrawniest horses Nathaniel had ever seen. They were good stock but hungry.

"Damn! Pardon, Miss, little lady," Nathaniel said. "This'll make it a bit harder to buffalo them but I'm not going to back out now."

As soon as the ladies were in back, Nathaniel spoke, "You're my wife and daughter and Red Wolf is your aged French father. *Parlez-vous, français?*"

Red Wolf chuckled, "*Oui.*"

Nathaniel switched out the horses' Indian tack for his own and put a blanket over each he then settled the girls in the back of his wagon and handed wrapped them in a blanket.

"You're feeling all-overish and might be coming down with pneumonia," Nathaniel said to Mary and Victoria, if I ask you something try and sound like a French lady or a white woman, but for Goodness sake do *not* sound like you've just come in to the reservation."

Victoria looked offended and Mary looked amused then said, "All-overish?"

"A little sick, feelin' poorly, not well, a cough maybe and a little fever."

"Oh, I see," Mary said, and both girls nodded.

"Here," Nathaniel pulled his rifle out of its scabbard. It was a new Centennial model Winchester lever action. "It's in .45-75 so it has a kick to it. It's not one of those pistol carbines you see."

Red Wolf nodded and said something that Mary translated, "He can shoot the buffalo-gun." Red Wolf took the rifle and years dropped away from him.

"Well *don't* unless I shoot first," Nathaniel said, "I'm going to try talking our way out of this. Just remember you're my French-Canadian wife and daughter."

"I won't forget, *mon père,*" Mary said mischievously.

"Nick, up in the wagon," Nathaniel said and swept his arm towards the wagon's seat. The big black wolfish dog leapt from the snow and sat on the seat on Nathaniel's left.

Nathaniel started the horses moving at a slow walk, he was afraid anything faster and the worn-out Indian ponies would be unable to keep up. Nathaniel checked the loads in his Greener and loaded the empty chamber in his pistols, he normally carried an empty chamber under the hammer to prevent misfires. He didn't have long to wait. Four men came riding at a quick trot up from the trail Nathaniel had taken that morning.

He kept the scattergun across his lap, but his hands were on the reins. Nick started his rumbling growl, "Hush." Nathaniel admonished the dog.

"Morning," Nathaniel said as the men caught up to him, "You're moving awful fast on this slick day. I'd slow down don't want your horse to come up with a broke leg."

"Mind your own business," a surly looking man in a woolen coat and his hat tied down with a long scarf around his chin declared.

"Did you see any Injuns on the trail?" another man asked. He was shorter than the first with a snow-burned red face and thick mittens with the fingers worn through.

"Nope, minding my own business. 'Fraid I didn't see anything."

"Don't get smart—" the man began when he saw both barrels of the shotgun pointing at his middle.

"I'm sorry, I'm a bit hard of hearing," Nathaniel said with a polite look on his face, "However, my wife and daughter are feeling poorly and trying to rest under a buffalo robe I got in back. So, I would appreciate it if you kept it down a bit."

"Sorry big guy," an older graying man on a bay gelding said, "We're looking for a couple of Injuns that have been wandering through here off the reservation. You know we had a whole bunch of people killed by those murdering savages not three-four years back."

"I haven't seen anybody on the trail but we ain't moving fast."

One of the men let his horse wander back to look at the horses tethered at the back. "Hey Curly, these horses look like palousies."

"That's a good eye," Nathaniel said casually, "I got them cheap, the man said they were easy keepers and would fatten up on the range. He's a stinking liar."

The men laughed, "He's a horse-trader, isn't he? They lie easy as breathing."

"You that blacksmith from Michigan?" the Older man asked.

"Minnesota," Lee replied, "But I am a blacksmith. Nathaniel Lee."

"If you need work done, I'll be in Cottonwood for a bit then moving on to Lewiston if the snow breaks. I thought spring meant 'spring' not an excuse to dump another foot of snow on you."

"Welcome to the Idaho territory," 'snow-burn' said with a horse-laugh, "You don't like the weather, just wait a minute and you'll get something to suit you."

The four men started up the trail ahead of the wagon. "They'll be back in a bit," Nathaniel said grimly.

"You know how to handle a big scattergun?" he asked Victoria, "This is a cut-down ten gauge and it will kick and makes an almighty noise."

"I can shoot a shotgun," Victoria reached for the Greener and broke open the action checking the shells. "How many shells do you have?"

"A box under the seat, take these," Nathaniel said taking a handful of brass shotgun cartridges from his jacket pocket.

"I'm going up in the rocks to the left, you wear my coat and hat," he told Victoria.

"You take this," he said handing over his gun belt with his pistols to Red Wolf, "I'll take my Winchester with me. A pair of pop-guns won't do me any good from there any way." Mary translated, and Red Wolf handed over the rifle but not without a regretful sigh.

"You Missy," Nathaniel nodded to Mary, "You keep your head down and sit quiet. Nick will keep an eye on you for me." Mary nodded her eyes round.

"Why are you helping us?" Victoria asked.

Nathaniel paused, "Because I don't like bas— uh, bullies for one. The rest will have to wait until we deal with them."

"Just keep driving the team slow and easy like I was before, Mose and Jacob will go good and steady for you. The sun will be in their eyes riding back, so they'll have a hard time seeing it ain't me until they get up close. I don't think they'll try to shoot me, or you out of hand.

But they won't take no for an answer."

Nathaniel stuffed a box of cartridges in each jacket pocket. Nick whined wanting to go with his master. "No, boy. Stay."

The big smith took off at a surprising pace for a man his size and clambered up into the rocks. They were fifty yards up the trail and seventy-five from the trail itself. The wind blew through them hard and it was bitterly cold resting his elbows on them without a coat and just his wool jacket, but he did not have to wait long.

The four men came riding back at a swift trot, their long guns were in their hands resting on their hips. Nathaniel thumbed back the hammer on his Winchester and laid the sights on the rear horseman.

"Lee, you give up them Injuns! We know you have them with you," the gray-haired man shouted about thirty yards from his wagon. They still did not realize it was not him.

Nathaniel fired knocking the last man riding from his horse. The horse bolted as the rider slid from his back spoiling the aim of the men in front of him. Nathaniel shot the second man and the two that were left fired, one shot at the wagon and the other at the gun-smoke from Nathaniel's rifle. A ricochet flattened like a pie plate and spun whining uncomfortably close to Nathaniel.

The men were experienced fighters and spurred their horses to split up. One rode behind the wagon out of sight of Nathaniel. The other rode straight for the left side of the wagon firing at Victoria as his horse galloped towards her. She stood up straight and shrugged off the heavy coat. She screamed in rage and fear, Nathaniel could see her teeth white as the snow as she fired both barrels of the big shotgun at once. The long gout of smoke and flame caught the rider in the chest, and he somersaulted over the back of his horse his coat smoking, limp as a ragdoll. Victoria fell back over the seat into the interior of the wagon. Nathaniel hoped she was not hit and just the recoil had sent her tumbling.

A fusillade of pistol shots sounded, and Nick leapt from the back of the wagon. Nathaniel saw the dog race around the side then a long scream followed by hair-curling growls from the big dog.

Nathaniel was already running back to the wagon.

Mary was crying holding the wounded Red Wolf. The old man had both smoking pistols in his hand and the canvas cover of the wagon had a dozen or more smoking black holes in it. The back of the wagon was thick with the stench of blood and the gun-smoke that hung thick in the air. The old man had given as good as he had gotten. Red Wolf spoke, and Mary said, "Thank you. That was more than I hoped for. Keep my girls safe." The old man closed his eyes for the last time.

"How's your sister?" Nathaniel asked, and Victoria stood up still wearing Nathaniel's hat.

"I need to hold the shotgun a bit tighter," she said unsteadily. Seeing Red Wolf down and dying she began to cry.

Nathaniel went around to the side of the wagon and saw Nick still worrying at the throat of the downed man. "Leave it!" Nathaniel ordered, and the dog backed off watching the downed man carefully licking his chops. If the half-dozen bullet holes in his jacket would not have done it for him, the gaping red and white hole where his throat used to be would have put paid to the man.

Nathaniel went back to see if there was anything he could do for Red Wolf, but he had already stopped breathing.

"You ladies, okay? Did you get hit?"

"No," Mary said, "We're okay, but I think Victoria bumped her head."

"Keep an eye on her, I'll do what needs doing.

"We can't keep their horses or gear," Nathaniel said, "but between me and the wolves I can make it look like they caught up with Red Wolf and he done them in and they did the same."

Nathaniel arranged the bodies just off the trail in the rocks with Red Wolf's back to a boulder. He started a very small fire like a desperate man might make on a cold spring night to keep the chill out of his old bones.

"The wolves will be by tonight, might not be much left after that," Nathaniel said crossing himself and saying a silent prayer for all five men.

"Won't be the wolves that get to him first," Victoria said sitting up. She offered Nathaniel's hat back and he took it gratefully, but he waved her off when she started to take off his coat.

"Buncha big grizzlies up here," Victoria said, "They got good noses they'll be here before the afternoon's over."

"We'll move off a bit and change the canvas. Anybody sees those holes will know we were in a shooting," Nathaniel said before they headed out.

A few miles down the trail, Nathaniel swapped out the old cover with a new one folding the old one making sure the bullet holes were not visible, "I'll patch it with a good piece of canvas when I get the chance."

That was the last they heard of the event except for an article in the Lewiston Teller about grizzlies rampaging near Cottonwood. That same year a girl was killed by a grizzly in the Kooskia area, so it was no great stretch. Nobody found the grizzly that killed the girl, but three big grizzlies were killed southeast of Cottonwood.

Rather than leave on their own, Victoria and Mary seemed anxious to stay with Nathaniel as he moved from strike to strike following the miners. He never wanted to mine himself, Nathaniel made his money off the miners themselves and did not do badly at all.

"It's been two years now," Victoria said as they set up house at a camp called, 'Winona'. Nathaniel and Victoria posed as man and wife and Mary as their child.

"Two and a half," Nathaniel remarked as he sat a chest he had made for Mary's clothes and things in her room. The house had two bedrooms, a sitting room, and a wood stove for heating and cooking. He had bought it half-finished from a man who had enough and finished it quickly improving it for the ladies.

"You and I pretend to be husband and wife," Victoria said.

"Yes," Nathaniel nodded quietly. The camp was not small, and the house was not too close to any neighbors, but it wasn't information that Nathaniel wanted known.

"Then what is wrong?" Victoria asked frustrated. She was wearing a gingham blue dress she had sewn herself that winter. Nathaniel thought it brought out the shine in her eyes.

"What's wrong with what?"

"Don't you want to get married for real? Is there something wrong with me?" Victoria looked worried, "You're not already married, are you?"

"I was," Nathaniel said quietly. "My wife and daughter died in the war."

"I'm sorry," Victoria replied. The house was quiet, and they could hear the bustle of the camp and the men working on the flue.

"So, do you not like me?"

"Of course, I like you and Mary," Nathaniel replied, "I've kept you both safe and sound, haven't I?"

"It's just, I've been alone a long time before I met you. That's part of it, but mostly I don't want to think you're obligated."

Victoria took his giant rough hands in her own, "Nathaniel Lee, you are obligated to me!" she gave him a sly smile. "All these years I've been cooking, and cleaning and I am nineteen years old. I am a spinster, you've taken my best years. You owe it to me, I am almost too old to have children now."

And so, they were married, a Catholic priest was making his way to Boise from Coeur d'Alene and was delighted to hold the services. Father Benoit spent a bit more time that was necessary on the importance of marriage, but he enjoyed chatting with the French-Canadian ladies.

They had settled into genuine domestic tranquility. Nathaniel was well respected and necessary being a skilled craftsman as well as willing to feed a man who was down on his luck. Victoria and Mary were treated like the queen and princess of the camp. No man offered them offense or insult, not the least reason was Nathaniel was the strongest man in the camp if not the territory.

That summer turned into fall and Nathaniel found he was going to be a father again, although he already felt that way towards Mary. The camp was not doing as well, some men claimed its luck had run and that it was time to move on.

"I think we should stay," Victoria said while she took laundry off the line, "Where is Mary? Always vanished when it is time to bring the wash in."

"She gets to playing," Nathaniel smiled while he trimmed a mule's hooves. Button was an easy animal to work on and he could have held a conversation even if the mule had been mean-spirited.

"Stay," Nathaniel gently tapped the mule to get her to lift her hoof, "Why would we stay? When the camp moves to the next strike, I pack up and go. It's how I've made my money for, well since the war ended."

"Stuart is a nice little town," Victoria said waving her hand vaguely north, "and there's always somebody wanting to trade."

Nathaniel worked for a bit humming to himself, trying to find the right words, "Victoria my heart, Stuart is getting played out, and even if it wasn't there will only be a few people living here after the miners move on. And none of them will have much cash money or real ore to trade."

"Because they are Indians," Victoria replied.

"Yes, because they are Indians. And they ain't miners nor farmers no matter what the Army wants them to be. What will they pay us with? Trapping isn't quite played out but it's not enough to make a living off and it's more hit and miss lately than mining. Their idea of farming is to dig up camas with a sharp stick. It's been a couple of years since they started trying

67

to plow anything. They work hard, everybody says so, but it takes more than just hard work to make a farm work. The nice Palousie horse is getting bred to some of the sorriest looking plow-mares I have ever seen, it's a crime."

"That is what we can do!" Victoria said, "We can be horse traders as well as farrier and blacksmith."

It was hard speaking sometimes because Nathaniel might look like an ogre, but he was a kind man. He didn't want his wife to feel badly or be discouraged.

"Missus Lee, these Indians just lost an almighty lot of good horses. Lots were killed, more were stolen, the Army's making them breed their stallions to draft mares," Nathaniel finished trimming the hoof and stood gently patting the mule on the back, "A good Palousie horse can fetch up to five, six hundred dollars. Even were I to find good horses to trade, nobody could or would buy them out here.

"People want a good mule like this Button here more than they do a saddle horse out here."

"Doesn't every man out here need a saddle horse?"

"Need? No not really, most men want them though," Nathaniel grew thoughtful. *When a man decides he's done he sells his mule though or he lets him go*, Nathaniel thought.

"If I let it be known I buy and sell..." the big man mused.

By the end of the week he was buying up mules and horses that miners were looking to sell. He did not pay much, but most of the men would have turned the animals loose rather than find pasturage or feed for them and the extra cash or goods as they left the camp allowed them to set themselves up better where they were going next.

Quickly though men began coming to Lee when they sold out often taking much less than Nathaniel thought was fair, he was tempted to offer more as his first offer for a horse because his conscience was bothering him.

"Why do you need to sell your burro, Tommy?" Nathaniel asked, "Pancho's a sweet little thing."

"He's too slow," Tommy Alistair replied grimly.

Nathaniel looked at Tommy quizzically, Tommy's pale blue eyes and grizzled beard and hair made him look older than his thirty years. He could have been anything between forty and sixty by looking at him.

"Haven't you heard her, in the evening?" Tommy asked low and quiet. Some men had a knack for bringing out the truth. Lee was one of those men, his size and strength and quiet demeanor gave him an air of trustworthiness.

"The Dusk woman the Indians are talking about her."

"Who?" Nathaniel asked. A chill ran down his spine, but he couldn't say why.

"She's some kind of spook woman," Tommy said, "Sounds like a cougar, but she takes folks in the night, children mostly."

Nathaniel laughed, "You've been hitting the hooch too hard."

"I've heard cougar, they're thick in these parts. There's still bear and wolf too, but I don't believe in spooks or haunts."

"Still, I'll give you a good price for Pancho," Nathaniel said.

Victoria was at the south fork of the river doing the laundry. It was something every woman had to do unless she hired it done. Victoria had made a few extra coins doing laundry for miners before the camp started to thin out. *I wish Mary was here, the work always seems to go faster*, Victoria thought.

Victoria heard footsteps behind her on the rocks the footsteps were light but careful, a woman or child carrying something. She heard the rustle of clothing and a package near her. Matilda, one of the Indian women from the camp joined her. "I see you have the best spot on the river," Matilda joked.

"Only the best for my husband's drawers," Victoria laughed back. It was a relief to have someone to talk to while she worked.

"It is getting to be the gray season here," Matilda said after a bit. "Make sure you and your little one are inside before the sun goes down."

"Why?" Victoria rubbed her husband's shirt against the washboard. *Pleasant but not as nice as when they play the washboard with a fiddle and a Jews' harp*, she thought.

"The gray time is coming when the mist comes up off the river at night and the rains fall, makes it dark early," Matilda said, "That's when the dusk woman comes."

"Who's the dusk woman?"

"She's a blind giant. She's old as old, comes in the dusk, at night when the mist comes. She takes children if she can back to her home up the mountain across the river in her cedar-root sack."

"Takes children?"

"Takes them and covers their eyes in pitch to make them blind like her. Then she eats them."

"Is this true?" Victoria asked skeptically.

"We don't talk about her when it gets dark out especially not across the river."

The women finished their laundry in silence, Matilda avoided looking across the river up the hill, but Victoria's gave was drawn there to the dark forested slope.

The mist came thick from where the two branches of the Clearwater came together. It crept up from the river and filled the ravines and hollows. "Come in now Mary," Victoria called down towards the creek.

Victoria stood at the edge of the corral watching the fog move up from the river. "Mary, time to come in," Victoria called urgently. A shape moved in the mist, tall, taller than Nathaniel or any man Victoria had ever seen or heard of. A weird call like a panther came from the thickening mist and the horses in the corral screamed bucking and rearing in place, crow-hopping and kicking their heels.

Something snapped in Mary, seeing the horses panic, she ran for the house and dashed past her sister. The figure was more a suggestion of light and mist than anything Victoria could say was there for sure but looking at it directly and it disappeared.

She quickly shut and bolted the door anyway. She looked out the small window and saw Nathaniel holding an oil lantern calming the horses. Nick stood next to Nathaniel, but his tail was low, and he was hunkered to the ground. Victoria had never seen Nick scared of anything, not even the big bears that ranged the edge of the camp in the spring. The tall shape vanished in the light of the lantern and the scream of a panther sounded from down the ravine towards the river. Victoria came grabbed the rifle from where it rested on its pegs and ran out the back door, "Stay inside," she told Mary as she dashed to her husband's side.

"Thanks," he said taking the rifle and handing her the lantern. "Is Mary inside?"

"Yep, I told her to stay there."

"Good. Whoa now," he said gently. "Whoa, easy there."

The horses settled at Nathaniel's voice but were still frightened, sweat mixed with the mist and poured down their backs as they quivered.

"Did you see who it was?" Victoria asked.

"Who what?" he asked distracted.

"Who was standing in the wash."

"No one, I don't think. There's a catamount out there. Didn't you hear it?"

"That wasn't a cougar, Nathaniel. It was the dusk woman."

"Dusk woman?"

"It's what the local Indians call her," Victoria said.

Nathaniel recognized the sound of superstition when he heard it, "It's nothing but an old mountain lion. Let's get inside." Nathaniel shooed his wife back towards the house but kept his attention towards the ravine as he returned to the house.

"Mary?" Victoria called as she came in the door, but there was no answer.

"Mary?" Nathaniel said loudly, but nothing no sound at all. The fire guttered in the hearth and Victoria's lantern flickered.

Nathaniel's eyes were round in his face, "I think the cat's got her it must have come in while we were out at the corral."

Nick began barking furiously at the doorjamb. "What's out there?" Nathaniel asked.

"No, look!" Victoria said pointing. On the doorjamb was black tar-like substance thick and slowly oozing down the jamb. It was a handprint, bigger than Nathaniel's giant hand print. Or part of a print because the doorjamb was too small for a whole print that size.

Nathaniel grabbed his gun belt and wrapped it around Victoria's thickening middle.

"You're going to need that," she protested.

"No, you'll have it and the scattergun. I've got my Winchester and these," Nathaniel held up a beaded belt holding a long bowie knife and an old tomahawk.

"You wait here in case she comes back," he wrapped the beaded belt around his waist and settled them around his hips. "Nick and I will bring her back."

"Com'on Nick," he said slapping his leg.

The big dog shivered like the horses, his eyes rolling, and he whined but he headed out the door into the thickening darkness.

Nathaniel waited until Victoria shut the door and he heard the latch slide home before he followed Nick into the mist. For all of Nathaniel's size he was silent when he moved in the forest. The dog and man hurried down the ravine. Nathaniel had his oil lantern and while the mist was moving in, he could still follow the trail. Half way down the ravine he found scuff marks like something made of rough cloth had scrapped against the ravine sides. Something being carried downhill.

At the water's edge he was able to follow twisted and turned rocks along the river bank to the river's edge. The track was steady and straight, and Nick did not waiver even though he never stopped shaking. Nick was not really 'Nick' he was Ol' Nick named for Satan himself. He had been like the devil himself and half wolf and feared neither man nor beast, but he was afraid of what they were following.

Across the river, Nathaniel could hear something in the water, something going on two legs by the sound. Stealthy steps but nothing was perfectly stealthy walking in a river. A sound came like the scream of a panther again, and maybe a muffled cry, like a child in a sack. He raised his rifle but did not, could not shoot. In the dark he would just as likely hit Mary.

Nick whimpered like a child but went into the icy water with his master. They crossed the river together half hidden figures moved in the fog. Shapes that moved on their own with the breeze or the movement of the water. Nathaniel remembered the men he had killed in war and the men who had tried to kill him. The men he had held as they died and the men who had killed his wife and daughter while he was fighting in Virginia.

Lakota men had been hunting and stealing eggs and set off a war back in Minnesota. They killed the wife of their friend. They killed her and his daughter, he never wanted to learn more about what they had done before killing his girls or after but the mist along the river told him the story.

He saw his little daughter and his young wife waiting at the door waving at the hunting party. Men that had been by their cabin before, men who had traded for Nathaniel's knives and axes, the work of his hands. They used to brutalize his wife and little girl before and after they had killed them.

The mist whispered to him as did the river telling him all the indignities and pain they suffered, each cry was whispered to him like an endearment. Each shout and laugh as they tormented the mother and child were told to him in exquisite detail. Nick reached out and grasped the cuff of his master's shirt and dragged him out of the river.

Across the river was another world darker, deserted, Winona had played out earlier almost a year and a half since anyone had worked that side of the river. Nathaniel's boots were full of water, but he made no move to dump them out. He stood shivering for long seconds then followed the path before him unerringly. He could have followed it without his lantern or dog. He could have followed it blind.

Nathaniel turned off the lantern and left it at the edge of the path where it reached the hillside. The mist in the old camp stretched along the pathways and cuts like a maze or web among the low shrubs and tangled rocks leading into the dark evergreen trees. He moved through the gray cloying mist like a wraith. The mist caressed his body with a spider-light touch, chill and tentative.

Halfway up the hillside it changed, the trees grew darker and thicker and all evidence of mining and digging ended. The underbrush was thicker but faded and dying as if it were the end of winter rather than the beginning of autumn. An angry red light was seen through the trees ahead. It was not warm and welcoming, the light looked secretive and hateful like the first spot of smallpox before it spreads across the body. No longer afraid, Nick looked to be a different dog. Something happened crossing the river, he appeared to lose the capacity for fear. In the trees the light revealed itself to be firelight shining between the slats of an Indian plank built long house like the coastal communities often built.

Wood smoke was now mixed with the mist and twined and twirled around like woven cedar baskets. Cat-footing to the house, Nathaniel put one eye to the slat and looked through the gap. He saw the supports were draped with woven cedar sacks. All were empty save one, that one moved slowly. Nathaniel knew Mary was in that.

A shape tall and terrible walked by the fire, head and shoulder taller than Nathaniel long and lean. The hair was Medusa's own tangle of gray like a thorn bramble. The eyes were pits of black horror, vile pitch dripped down the valleys of her wrinkled face. She wore a filthy dress of woven cedar root like the sacks. She was at least eight feet tall and thin as a dead sapling. She tossed an armload of wood on the fire and sparks flared.

The blind woman turned and went to the door of the longhouse. She moved a thick door woven of flexible branches and grasses to one side and left silently into the darkness. Nathaniel could feel her presence as she walked into the mist.

He slipped into the hut, heavy benches framed the firepit. The support poles were old rotting up close. The heat from the fire cause the moisture in the logs to begin steaming in the longhouse. The rafters of the longhouse were filled with strips of drying smoked meat and carven masks full of pain and horror. The masks had lank hair most black as midnight but some lighter brown and even a couple blonde falls of tangled hair. Nathaniel reached up and lifted the bag with Mary down. He could not untie the tangled knot that held the bag shut but the razor edge of his bowie knife made short work of it. Nathaniel was horrified to see Mary's eyes had been glued shut with black pitch like the hag. Nick snarled like bones grinding in a bandsaw and she was there!

The dusk woman raised her fist high. Nathaniel thrust the barrel of his rifle into her middle it was like hitting the bole of a big fir tree. The dusk woman was unfazed by the blacksmith's strike and her return blow landed knocking Nathaniel to the ground. Mary was swept along with him and they tumbled behind her heavy carved cedar bench. The big dog leapt at the giantess knocking her back his ivory fangs locked in her narrow neck.

A devil in truth! The black dog looked purely savage now, no longer the friend and companion of years, he was a whirling, jerking mass of hate and fury. The catamount scream of the dusk woman sounded loud in the big longhouse. The two were locked in mortal combat on the edge of the firepit. Nathaniel found his feet and rushed the tall ogress knocking both her and his old friend into the roaring fire that arose to grab at them greedily.

Nathaniel looked over at one of the rotting support poles then using his massive strength struck it with a blow of his whole arm. The pole snapped crumbling at the top and fell into the fire trapping both the black dog and his now flaming foe. Nathaniel turned and picked up the slab of cedar the old monster used as a bench. Worn smooth over years, perhaps centuries it was as filled with rot as the post he snapped it free of its supports and lifted high overhead smashed across the firepit covering the head of both combatants.

The roof was groaning its warning, Nathaniel grabbed Mary up and rushed out of the now collapsing longhouse. He stopped just outside to take the pitch from Mary's eyes. The roof of the longhouse moaned like a dying man and with many loud cracks crashed into the now raging fire sending up a great cloud of sparks. The sparks whirled and swept through the mist with a malevolent hum. Several landed upon Mary and Nathaniel, the big man brushed them away, but they bit into Mary like mosquitoes and she swatted at them until he reached out and smothered the last of them.

The trip home down the mountainside through the old camp and across the river was a nightmare. Crossing the river, Nathaniel swept up the young girl and cradled her in his arms like a babe. Her eyes glinted in the darkness like stars in the cold winter sky.

He hollered at the edge of the ravine to let Mary know it was him. She was waiting at the door with the Greener clasped tight. She waited until she saw both their faces clearly before she set it aside to hug her sister and husband.

Mary looked at the swell of her sister's belly and the burning pain of the longhouse's embers stung her again with the memory of their fiery bite. She could hear her sister and Nathaniel speaking out endearments and reassurances but all she felt was fierce hunger as she listened to the beat of the baby's heart.

Who was that masked author?

Josephine's Revenge

Damito Huffman

Josephine Walker rode into Rattler's Ridge in a cloud of dust on the back of her trusty steed, Merlin. She was hell bent on killing the man who gunned down her father on their ranch. She was told in the last town that Edward "Colt" Haskell was heading here. Women and children ran to get out of her way. She drew her horse to a stop in front of the local saloon.

She dismounted in a swish of satin and lace. Tying Merlin to the hitching post, she clunked across the boardwalk up to the saloon doors. She pushed open the doors with a swish and entered the building. It always amazed Josephine how quiet a saloon was during the day. There were a few old timers sitting around swapping stories. The piano player wasn't sitting on his bench, but the automatic player was on so music floated through the air. Josephine made her way to the bar. A middle-aged man stood behind the bar wiping a glass with a towel. He nodded in her direction.

"What'll it be ma'am?"

Josephine took time to stretch her back while holding onto the bar. "Beer and a room."

"I can give you the beer, but I don't have any empty rooms." He reached under the bar for a glass, filled it with beer, and slid it over to Josephine.

Josephine raised her eyebrows at him. "No rooms?" She brought the glass to her lips and took a long swig of the beer.

"Nope, sorry. The few rooms I had got taken yesterday."

"Oh, well, then, where could I get a room?"

"You might try Miss Etta's place. She owns the General Store. She has some rooms that she rents out from time to time. It would be better suited for a lady like you."

Josephine laughed a hearty laugh. "Don't judge a book by its cover, Mister."

Marcus nodded. "You can find Miss Etta's place just down the road on the right. She'll be the little lady behind the counter. Tell her Marcus sent you. She'll be able to get you whatever you need."

"Thank you, sir. What do I owe you for the beer?"

"You're new in town, this one's on me."

Josephine nodded. "Thanks again, Marcus. I'll see you around."

Josephine smiled at Marcus, tipped her hat, turned on her heel, and left the saloon. She walked out into the bright sunlight. She looked around getting a feel for this little town. There were children playing in the street. Dogs ran after the children nipping at their heels. Women carried baskets of eggs and homemade preserves along with cages with chickens to barter for other goods. Josephine noticed the bank across the street along with the jail just a few doors down. She smiled to herself thinking how convenient that must be.

Three buildings to the left of the jail, with a huge sign above it that read "General Store," sat a two-story white-washed building. Josephine started off toward the store when she was stopped short by a horse and rider. She jumped backwards onto the boardwalk to avoid being trampled. Her heel caught on a crack in the wood and she fell on her backside, hard.

"Damn! That's gonna leave a mark."

The rider of the horse jumped down and ran to Josephine. "I'm sorry ma'am. Allow me to help you up." He extended his hand to Josephine.

Josephine looked up but couldn't see anything with the sun glaring in her eyes. Angrily she batted away his hand. "I can get up on my own."

"Do you need a doctor?"

"No, I'm fine. My pride is just a bit bruised."

Josephine stood up and brushed the dust off her dress. She turned toward her adversary. "Thank you for not killing me." With that she gathered up her dress and headed off across the street toward the general store leaving the kind stranger staring bewildered after her.

Miss Etta had given Josephine the best room in the house or so she said. Josephine didn't travel with baggage so instead of having clean clothes to change into, she just bought a new dress in every town. She would have the dirty one cleaned and shipped back to her ranch. This would make the eighth dress that would be waiting for her when she got home. She missed her ranch, especially her ranch hand Little Joe. She knew her ranch was in good hands. She made a mental note to send a telegram home to let the men know where she was and if things went her way, she would be home soon. She bounced down the stairs to find Miss Etta in the kitchen.

"Good morning, Miss Etta."

"Good morning, Josephine. Did you sleep well?"

"Yes, ma'am, is there anything I can help you do?"

"No, I'm just finishing up the eggs. Pour yourself a cup of coffee and sit down at the table."

Josephine took a coffee mug out of the cabinet and poured herself a cup of coffee. She walked back to the table and sat down. Folding a napkin across her lap, she brought the cup to her nose and took a long sniff. She loved the smell of coffee. The taste was even better. She took a small sip and relished as the hot liquid slid down her throat.

"There's nothing like hot coffee in the morning." Josephine said behind her steaming mug.

"I used to only drink tea until my late husband Charlie got me used to it. He had me hooked the first time I took a sip. I've never looked back."

"I'm sorry, Miss Etta. How'd he die, if you don't mind my asking?"

"He was gunned down while unloading a supply wagon. Never did find his killer."

Josephine gasped. This was too close to home for her. "Oh, Miss Etta, how awful. I am so sorry for bringing it up."

Loretta "Etta" Tucker reached across the table and patted Josephine's hand. "Honey, it's alright. He left me a long time ago. I've learned to go on and do without him. I've got a good son and workers that come in and help out. I couldn't make it through the day without them."

Josephine smiled a sad smile. "I can relate to those feelings."

"You lose your husband, honey?"

"No, my father. We have a ranch out in the west of Texas. He was gunned down about six months ago just because he wouldn't sell his prize horse."

Etta looked at Josephine's shining eyes. "You've come to seek revenge for his death haven't you, honey?"

Josephine looked Miss Etta in the eye. "Yes, yes I have. I've heard he's here in Rattler's Ridge. If I get the chance, I will put a bullet right in the middle of his heart. He was a coward and shot my daddy in the back. I want to watch his eyes as my bullet shoves its way into his skin."

Miss Etta gasped. "Honey, you shouldn't talk like that. Ladies shouldn't

82

Josephine's Revenge

have that much anger inside them."

"Miss Etta, I don't claim to be a lady. I've helped my daddy on the ranch since I was old enough to walk. My mom died of pneumonia when I was only ten. I've always carried my own weight."

Miss Etta patted Josephine's hand once again. "Well, sounds like you've got your mind made up on this. I've never been one to stick my nose into other people's business."

Josephine and Etta cleared the table and washed the dishes in companionable silence. Josephine put the dishes away and turned to Miss Etta.

"Miss Etta, I don't want you to think I'm not civilized. My daddy raised me with manners and to respect others. I can be as genteel as the next but I'm not going to let Edward "Colt" Haskell get away with murder any longer."

Josephine watched Miss Etta visibly stiffen. "Who did you say?"

"Edward "Colt" Haskell. Why? Wait, was he the one that shot your husband?"

Tears were swimming in Miss Etta's eyes. Her voice quivered as she spoke. "Is he really back in town?"

"That's what I was told."

Miss Etta reached for a chair. Josephine grabbed her around the waist and helped her sit down.

"Miss Etta, I'm so sorry. I didn't mean to upset you. I didn't know."

Miss Etta dabbed at her eyes with a handkerchief she pulled from her pocket. "It's okay. It's been ten years. I really should let it go. What scares me the most is if my son knows he's back in town, he'll go after him, too."

"I promise not to say a word to anyone about why I am here. I wouldn't even know your son if he came up and said hello."

Miss Etta smiled and nodded. "If you are going to be around here for a little while, he's supposed to come help me restock the top shelves. I can

83

introduce you to him."

"I was going to go out and see if I could spot "Colt". You know, see what he does during the day. Where he hangs out. That sort of thing. It can wait for a few hours, I suppose."

Just as Josephine finished talking, they heard the back door open and close, followed by heavy footsteps coming down the hall. Josephine turned toward the sound. Miss Etta walked to the door, unlocked it, and turned the closed sign to open. She opened the door and pushed a huge barrel of potatoes in front of it to keep it open.

"That barrel is bigger than you. You should have asked me to do that."

Miss Etta propped her hands on her hips. "Why would I ask you to do something I have been doing for over 25 years? Just because I am short, doesn't mean I can't take care of myself."

"I'm sorry, Miss Etta. I didn't mean to offend you."

The man who had been coming down the hall walked over to Miss Etta, grabbed her around the waist, twirled her around a few times, and kissed her on the cheek.

"Alonzo, put me down this instant." Miss Etta said with a smile. She grabbed his face between her hands and kissed him on the tip of his nose.

"Hello, Mom. How are you?"

"I'll be better when you put me down."

Alonzo eased his mom down. "Now, what was it you needed me to help you with today?"

"I need those shelves restocked with boots and I got a new shipment of spices and soaps. If you can do the boots, I can take care of everything else."

"You got it mom. By the way, who's the woman that's been staring at me?"

Miss Etta turned around. "Oh, goodness, I forgot about you, Josephine. Josephine Walker I'd like you to meet my son, Alonzo Tucker."

Alonzo reached out his hand to shake Josephine's. "She didn't want me to help her yesterday; I don't see why she would shake my hand today."

Josephine frowned. When did he offer to help her yesterday? Horror filled her face when she remembered the stranger that almost ran her over with his horse.

"It was you? You were the crazy man on his horse that almost ran over me? I have a huge bruise on my hip from that fall."

Alonzo dropped his hand back to his side. "I told you yesterday I was sorry. I gave Jack his reins and he got a little carried away. I didn't get him reined in fast enough. He wouldn't have hit you, he just likes beautiful women. He's just a big baby."

"It scared the crap out of me."

Miss Etta was standing there looking between the two. "What did you do to her, Alonzo?"

"I didn't do anything, Mom. I just gave Jack a little too much freedom. He saw Josephine and you know how he is with beautiful women. He ran toward her a little too fast and spooked her a bit. She jumped back and fell. I apologized and offered to help her up. She refused my offer and that was that."

"You caused her to fall?"

"No, Jack did."

"You were on Jack. He was your responsibility."

Alonzo hung his head. There was no use in trying to argue with a woman whose ancestry goes back to Holland and Germany. She had a stubborn streak a mile long. For a woman who only stood four foot nine and weighed 90 pounds on a good day, she could hold her own with the biggest town drunk and had.

"Yes, ma'am." He looked at Josephine. "I deeply apologize, Miss Walker. I didn't mean to scare you yesterday. I wasn't lying; Jack does go a bit crazy when he's around beautiful women. Please accept my sincerest apologies."

Josephine couldn't help but smile at this man who clearly stood over six feet tall but was being berated by his mom in front of a complete stranger. She extended her hand toward Alonzo.

"Look, I'm sorry. I was new in town, tired, and dirty. I had been riding almost nonstop for two days. I just wanted to find a place to stay where I could get cleaned up and eat. I have a quick temper and you just happen to be the target of mine yesterday. Truce?"

Alonzo smiled back at Josephine. "I'll accept your apology if you accept mine."

They shook hands and at the same time they said. "Deal."

Josephine, Etta, and Alonzo worked together in companionable silence for several hours. Josephine hadn't felt this good in months. It felt good to be doing manual labor again. She hadn't realized how much she missed working until now. She was anxious to get back to her ranch. Josephine finished organizing the new soaps. She went to Miss Etta to see if she needed help with the spices.

"I'm finished with the spices. Alonzo why don't you show Josephine around our little town?"

Alonzo and Josephine's heads snapped up and looked at Miss Etta. They both said, "What?"

"Miss Etta, I'm sure Alonzo has better things to do than show a visitor around town."

Alonzo wanted to get to know Josephine better but wasn't about to push himself on her. She had made it very clear she didn't want to have anything to do with him. He looked at her and wondered what in her life had caused her to be so jaded.

Miss Etta smiled to herself. She had seen the look in Alonzo's eyes. He was intrigued by Josephine and if Miss Etta had anything to do with it, she would have Josephine doing all sorts of things to keep her mind off revenge.

"I could take you to the stables and introduce you to Jack. You'll see he's a sweetheart."

"I suppose that will be okay. I need to go check on Merlin anyway. I'll buy an apple from Miss Etta to give to him."

Miss Etta looked at Josephine and Alonzo. "Take Merlin and Jack both an apple. Give Jack my love."

Alonzo offered his arm to Josephine. She did a small curtsy, accepted his arm and let him lead her out back to the stable. Miss Etta's eyes sparkled when she saw them walk outside arm in arm.

Alonzo held the door open for Josephine. As soon as he was out the door, he offered Josephine his arm again. They walked in silence each lost in their own thoughts.

When they reached the stable, they heard the bell over the door clang. They looked back toward the store. Josephine looked questioningly at Alonzo.

"She's run the store for 25 years. She can handle herself."

"Okay, if you are sure. I've just got a gut feeling that something is wrong."

"We can go back if you want. I don't want to be on the receiving end of her temper."

"Miss Etta has a temper?"

"Yes, ma'am, she keeps it in check most of the time. Are you really worried about her?"

"Yes, I am. I don't know why but I just feel like something bad is going to happen."

"Okay, let's go."

Josephine and Alonzo walked back to the store. Alonzo motioned for Josephine to stay behind him. Josephine reached into her dress pocket and wrapped her hand around her gun. She always carried a Webley Bull Dog, fully loaded and ready to go at all times.

Alonzo paused in the kitchen. He reached into a cabinet above the stove. He brought out a Winchester .44/40 rifle. He grabbed a box of bullets from the same cabinet. He loaded the gun and shoved the rest of the bullets in his pants pocket.

He slowly made his way down the hall toward the front of the store. They could hear voices coming from the front. They both stopped when they heard Miss Etta's voice rise above all them.

"If you rabble-rousers aren't going to buy anything, I'm going to have to ask you to leave."

"That's not very friendly now is it ma'am? I don't take too kindly to being talked to like that. You don't want to make me mad."

Alonzo reached out and turned a door knob to Josephine's right. He nodded for her to go in. She and Alonzo quietly went inside. To Josephine's surprise there was a hidden room that was right behind the shelves behind the counter. What looked like a mirror to the customers was actually a two-way mirror. Alonzo and Josephine watched six guys moving around the store. The guys were beginning to circle Miss Etta. She kept backing up toward the counter. Miss Etta put her hand in her pocket.

Alonzo leaned over and whispered in Josephine's ear. "Mom keeps an Apache Revolver in her pocket. It is only effective if they get right up on her. If they get close enough to touch her, she'll shoot them in the gut."

Josephine shivered when Alonzo's breath brushed her ear. She smiled to herself. Miss Etta really could take care of herself. Alonzo stuck the barrel of the Winchester into a hole in the mirror.

"Alonzo, what are you doing?" Josephine whispered.

"I'm defending my store. I won't shoot until they start something. I see one person put anything in their pocket or lay one hand on mom, I'll fire a warning shot into that target over the door. There's another rifle in that door right there if you want to use it." Alonzo nodded to a door just to Josephine's left.

Josephine opened the door and took out another Winchester rifle. She checked to see if it was loaded and it was. She looked around for a hole to stick the barrel through. Alonzo pointed to a place just to her left. She nodded and placed the barrel into the hole.

Josephine looked through the mirror and saw a block of wood above the door. It looked like it had been fired into a couple of times.

Miss Etta had kept her distance from the group. She had finally made it to the end of the counter.

Josephine leaned over and whispered in Alonzo's ear. "What is she doing?"

"There is a loaded Colt .45 Peacemaker under the counter."

"Smart."

Miss Etta kept her cool all through the barrage from the maniac. She never said anything back to him and she didn't get in his way. Her left hand was within reach of the Peacemaker. She leaned her hip against the counter.

Alonzo and Josephine waited. All the sudden one of the gang members picked up a jar of preserves and threw it to the ground. Josephine flinched and saw Miss Etta stiffen. Alonzo shifted his stance just slightly and took aim. Josephine noticed he wasn't aiming at the block of wood. Before she could react, another gang member reached out his arm and swept everything off the shelf he was standing at. Josephine didn't hesitate. She aimed her gun on him. She glanced sideways toward Alonzo. He nodded and pulled the trigger. Josephine pulled her trigger at the same moment. Both guys went down.

Miss Etta grabbed the Peacemaker from behind the counter and stuck it in the gut of the guy in front of her. The other three guys had pulled their guns but couldn't figure out where the shots had come from. They knew Miss Etta couldn't have shot them. They were wildly pointing their guns everywhere. Alonzo and Josephine had already aimed their rifles on two of the three remaining.

"I'm only saying this once. Put your guns away and get out of my store and never come back."

The leader of the gang shook in anger. He pointed his finger in Miss Etta's face and pretended to shoot her. She didn't flinch.

"You better watch your back old woman. I'm coming for you and whoever is hiding behind that wall."

Miss Etta pulled the hammer back on the Peacemaker. "Don't ever threaten me or people I care about. Do you hear me, sonny? Leave now before you die here and now."

The stranger eased out of the store backwards. The other three members of his gang had already made their way outside. Alonzo and Josephine made their way out of the store room to Miss Etta. Alonzo grabbed his mom and hugged her tight.

"You did good, mom."

Miss Etta was shaking. Josephine took the Peacemaker out of her hand and placed it back behind the counter.

"I thought you two were in the stable?"

Josephine placed her hand on Miss Etta's shoulder. "I'm sorry, Miss Etta, I just had a gut feeling that something bad was going to happen. I made Alonzo come back."

Miss Etta patted Josephine's hand. "I'm actually glad you did. I'm not saying I couldn't have handled them, but they did scare me. I need to get the Sheriff and let him know what happened."

Alonzo nodded. "I'll go."

Josephine saw the mess the hoodlums had made. "I guess I'll start cleaning this up."

"No, don't. Not before the Sheriff comes. He needs to see what they did. We have to show him it was self-defense."

Josephine nodded. "How about I get us some coffee?"

"That would be great."

By the time Josephine had brought out two cups of coffee, Alonzo was back with the Sheriff.

The Sheriff took off his hat as he entered the store. He nodded toward Miss Etta.

"Hey, Miss Etta, I heard you've had some problems this morning."

"Nothing my son and this lovely woman didn't take care of."

The Sheriff looked at Josephine. She stepped forward and extended her hand. "Hello, Sheriff, I'm Josephine Walker. I just got into town yesterday. I'm sorry to cause problems in your town."

"Nice to meet you Miss Walker, I'm Sheriff Jarrod Barker. Shoot, you two took out two members of the Colt Gang."

Josephine took a few steps back. "Did you say Colt Gang? These were members of the Colt Gang?"

Alonzo, Josephine, and Miss Etta looked from one to the other. Miss Etta was the only one who knew Josephine's secret. Alonzo was the one who had fire in his eyes.

"That son of a bitch. Mom, you had the chance to shoot him and didn't. He killed dad for God's sake."

"Alonzo Tucker, you know I don't shoot unless I have to. I scared him off."

"Yeah but he said to watch your back. He said he was going to come back. Mom, I don't like this."

Sheriff Barker walked over to the two guys and checked for a pulse. "Miss Etta, did I hear you say Colt threatened you?"

"Yes, he did."

"Then if he sets foot back inside this store, you have every right to defend it by any means necessary. You can shoot on sight and nothing will be said. We've been after this gang for a long time. He's killed all over this territory. I'll deputize Alonzo so it will be even more legal."

"Whatever you feel like you need to do, Jarrod."

"Alonzo come down to the jail after you get this cleaned up and I'll get you deputized."

Alonzo nodded. "Thanks, Jarrod."

"I'll go get the undertaker."

A group of townspeople had gathered on the porch of the store. There were whispers going around that the beautiful stranger had killed two men with her bare hands. Josephine shook her head. It was so amazing how fast rumors got started and spread.

Alonzo hired a few of his friends to come help out at the General Store a few days each week when he had other things to keep him busy. Miss Etta fussed and fretted but Alonzo wouldn't take no for an answer. He had lost his dad to Edward "Colt" Haskell he was not going to lose his mom to the same killer.

Josephine hung close to Miss Etta as well. The only time she left Miss Etta was when she went to the stable to brush Merlin. She was in the stable brushing and talking to Merlin one day when Alonzo walked in. Alonzo didn't want to bother her, so he stayed behind the stack of hay.

"Merlin, I'm sure you miss the other horses especially Lancelot and Midnight. I'm sure they miss you, too. Hopefully we'll be home soon. If I know Colt Haskell, he'll make his move sometime this week. He's not known for patience. It only took Daddy refusing to sell him Midnight for two months before he came and gunned him down." Merlin turned his head and nibbled at Josephine's hair. Josephine nuzzled Merlin's neck. "God, Merlin, I miss him so much. This pain isn't going away. I was hoping it would have eased up some by now. I just have so much anger built up inside me. I can still remember that day just like it was yesterday..."

Josephine was in the barn when she heard the gun shots ringing out across the valley. Normally she wouldn't think anything about hearing a gun-shot but the Colt Gang had been trying to get her father to sell them his retired racehorse, Midnight. They claimed they wanted to stud him out so he could sire them a winner. Josephine's father, Garrett Walker knew they were not going to sire him but put him back on the track. He didn't want Midnight mistreated. He wanted him to live out his retirement in peace. Garrett would take the old horse out daily for a leisurely stroll. He let Midnight have his reins when he felt the old horse needed to run.

Garrett had been mending fences on the back forty all morning with most of the ranch hands. Edward "Colt" Haskell wasn't a man who took "no" for an answer. He got what he wanted and didn't care how he got it. He had killed for less.

Josephine grabbed her gun and jumped on Merlin. She headed toward her father. She never once stopped to think about the danger she was heading into. She knew she had to get to her father and fast. Josephine and Merlin headed into the thickets. Garrett didn't like Josephine going into them because of all the rattlesnakes that lived in their depths. Josephine wasn't worried about being bit by a snake, she was only thinking about her father. She and Merlin burst through the thicket to see the back side of

Colt's horse heading over the ridge along with a volley of gunfire from the ranch hands. Her father was laying on the ground in a pool of blood. She slid off of Merlin and ran to her father's side. She ripped apart one of her petticoats and pressed it into his wound.

"Josey, I'm sorry." Derrick, one of the ranch hands placed his hand on Josephine's shoulder. "They got the drop on us."

"It's okay. He's going to be okay."

Garrett gave a gargling laugh. "Don't lie child. I'm dying. I know it. You know it. They know it. I don't want to die out here. Get me back to the house."

"Sure, Dad.

Three of the ranch hands eased Garrett up into a sitting position. Garrett let out a groan. Little Joe walked up to Garrett and picked him up as if he weighed nothing. He sat him down on Merlin's saddle.

"Take Mr. Garrett home, Merlin."

Little Joe was not a man to be messed with. He stood six foot eight inches tall and weighed in at over 300 pounds. He was a little slow in learning but had a heart as big as the entire unsettled west. He turned to Josephine.

"I go find Roscoe and bring him home."

Josephine nodded her thanks to the men. They went back to work as Josephine jumped into the saddle of her dad's horse, Lancelot, and followed Merlin back to their two-story farm house. Merlin took it slow and easy all the way. Josephine knew her father would be in and out of consciousness the entire way home. Merlin took Garrett straight to the porch. He stood extremely still and waited for Josephine.

Josephine helped Garrett down. He stumbled through the front door and collapsed on the floor. His breathing was fast and shallow.

"Daddy?"

Garrett raised his hand toward Josephine. She took his hand and placed it over her heart.

"Josey, promise me you won't avenge my death."

"Daddy, you know I can't do that."

"Yes, I know but I thought I would ask anyway. Could you just please humor your dying dad?"

Tears welled up in Josephine's eyes. "I'm sorry, Daddy. I can't make you that promise. You know I love you more than life itself."

"I know, Josey. I love you, too."

Garrett took a few more breaths and died holding his beloved daughter's hand. Josephine held onto her father's hand and cried until no more tears came. She placed his hands on his chest and closed his eyes. She stood up, wiped her tear stained face, and headed toward the barn. Merlin and Lancelot followed at her heels. Josephine reached up and patted Merlin's neck without thinking. Merlin nibbled at her hair. Josephine took Merlin's and Lancelot's saddles and blankets off and gave them both a quick brushing. She opened their stalls and both horses walked inside. Josephine didn't bother locking the stalls as they could open the doors themselves. Both horses knew where they needed to be. Josephine took the saddle soap and a rag from the tack shelf and cleaned the blood from her saddle.

Little Joe had found Roscoe hiding under one of the beds in the bunkhouse. Roscoe had followed Little Joe around while he had dug Garrett's grave all by himself. The other workers had finished up their daily chores and made their way back to the barn. Roscoe came trotting up to Josephine with his tail tucked between his legs. Josephine smiled a sad smile at Roscoe and bent down to give him a scratch behind the ears.

Little Joe came forward, "Miss Josey, I is sorry about Mr. Garrett. I found Roscoe hiding in the bunkhouse then I dugged Mr. Garrett's grave."

Josephine looked up at Little Joe, "All by yourself?"

Little Joe nodded, "Yes ma'am."

"Well, thank you, Little Joe. He's in the house. I need to make him a coffin."

Derrick stepped forward, "No need, Miss Josephine. I had a couple of the greenhorns take care of that."

Josephine nodded, "Well, it looks like everything has been taken care of except laying Daddy to rest."

The farm hands followed Josephine back to the main house. They walked inside to see him laying right where Josephine had left him. The greenhorns drove the wagon up to the front porch with the coffin in the back. Little Joe took his hat off, walked over to Garret and picked him up like you would a tiny kitten. He carried Garrett out to the coffin and placed him gently inside. Little Joe placed his hand on Garrett's head.

"I loved you, Mr. Garrett. You have been like a father to me."

Josephine choked back a sob. "He loved you, too, Little Joe. In fact, he thought of all of you like his children instead of just hired hands. You were his equals."

All the workers filed by the coffin to pay their respects before placing the lid on and nailing it in place. They followed the wagon to the grave Little Joe dug and lowered it by the ropes that were attached to the handles. Josephine recited Garrett's favorite Psalm and they all sung his favorite song "Amazing Grace". Everyone took a turn throwing a shovel full of dirt into the grave. Little Joe went last and finished covering the coffin of their beloved boss. The sun was just beginning to set sending shades of pink, orange, and purple across the sky. This was normally Josephine's favorite time of day but today the sky had lost all its beauty.

Josephine collapsed in a heap of emotions at Merlin's feet. Alonzo's heart broke for Josephine. She had put on such a brave face when she was falling apart inside. He went to Josephine. Merlin raised his head up and nudged Alonzo's arm. He smiled to himself. He had spoiled the horse since he'd been here. Alonzo put his hand into his pocket and brought out some sugar cubes for Merlin. He held them under the horse's nose. Merlin ate them quickly. Alonzo walked to Merlin's side where Josephine had collapsed.

He sat down beside her and placed an arm around her shoulders. Without thinking Josephine laid her head on Alonzo's shoulder. Alonzo pulled out a handkerchief and handed it to Josephine. She took it, wiped her eyes, and blew her nose.

"Thank you."

"You're welcome. Feeling better?"

"Not really. Will I ever get over him?"

"No."

"Seriously?"

"I have days that I still miss my Dad. It doesn't ever go away. Some days are better than others. You just have to take it one day at a time and find things you love to do."

"So, seeking vengeance was a bad idea?"

"Probably, but I understand where you are coming from. With Colt in town and gunning for my mom, I'm sure one of us will take him down."

Josephine nodded against his shoulder. "How much longer do you think we are going to have to wait?"

"Knowing Colt, not much longer."

"I just want this to be over so I can go home. I think I miss my ranch as much as I miss my Dad."

"I can understand that. If Mom hadn't had the store to keep her going, I'm not sure she would have survived this long."

"I've only known your mom for a little while, but I've grown to love her, too."

Alonzo leaned back against the wall with Josephine still on his shoulder. This just felt right. It felt comfortable. This is what had been missing in his life. He needed Josephine by his side.

Merlin whinnied and Josephine sat up straight, accidentally elbowing Alonzo in the ribs.

"Ow, that hurt."

Josephine tried to get to her feet. "I'm sorry, I didn't mean to hurt you. Something's wrong."

Josephine had been right about the first attack on his mom. He didn't hesitate, he got on his feet and helped Josephine up. They both took off running toward the store. They saw the smoke before they saw the flames.

"Oh, God, he's burning the store down."

Josephine had her Bull Dog out. Alonzo grabbed a gun from his saddle. He loaded it as he went. They saw two of Colt's gang setting fire to the back of the store.

Alonzo said, "Left."

Josephine understood what he meant. They each took aim on their men. They fired and hit their targets. The men fell before they could set the fire. Alonzo and Josephine yanked open the back door. A little ball of energy knocked Josephine down before she realized what was happening. Alonzo reached out and grabbed. He caught a handful of skirts.

Miss Etta was screaming for him to turn her loose. She had a broom in her hand and began hitting Alonzo over the head with it.

"Mom, mom, stop! It's me, Alonzo. Stop hitting me, please."

Miss Etta dropped her broom. "Sorry, son. I thought you were one of them."

"It's okay, mom. Where's the other ones. We got two more of them. That only leaves two."

"I don't know. They threw lit bottles of whiskey through the front windows. I don't know if we can even save anything."

"I'm not worried about the stupid store, mom. All I care about is you." Alonzo hugged his mother.

Josephine noticed movement out of the corner of her eye while Alonzo and Miss Etta talked. She eased to the side of store. Alonzo looked up.

"What's up?"

She shook her head and placed a finger over her lips. She pointed toward the side of the store. Alonzo low crawled toward the side of the building. There stood Colt and the last member of his gang, Dennis.

Many of the townspeople had started a bucket brigade to put out the fire. Colt thought they were out of sight and might have been to people in front. He was in plain sight to Josephine and Alonzo. Each one wanted him, and they knew they would have him. Josephine didn't want to shoot him in the back. She wanted to see his eyes when she shot him.

Josephine broke a stick that had been lying beside her on the ground. Colt turned around. He saw a man and woman standing there pointing a gun right at him. The look on his face was priceless.

He raised his arms in the air. "Hey, I'm not even armed."

"Neither was my father when you shot him in the back." Josephine said as she took a step forward.

"My dad was unloading a wagon when you shot him in the back. What's the matter too scared to face a man and shoot him while he's looking at you? You have to pick on a helpless old woman who is trying to make a living running a general store?"

"Hey, she started this. She yelled at me."

"Oh, boo-hoo, look at the big, brave man got his little feelings hurt by a woman who only stands four feet nine. Man up, for god's sake. Face up to all murders you've committed. It's time to face the music. Either draw or die as you are."

Dennis was trying to sneak away. Alonzo fired his gun into the air. He stopped short. He turned around slowly with his hands in the air. Josephine never took her gun off Colt.

"How do you want to do this, Alonzo?" Josephine asked.

"I say we do a quick draw and see who's left standing."

"Sounds good to me."

Colt and Dennis said at the same time, "I don't have a gun."

Miss Etta spoke up. "Sure, you do. You both have one stuffed in your boot. Pull them out and let's go."

Colt and Dennis looked at each other. They really were nothing but big bullies.

"Either you die trying or you just die. The choice is yours." Josephine stated.

"Alonzo and Josephine, you go stand over there. Colt and Dennis can stand over there. Everyone will drop their guns down by their sides. On the count of three, everyone bring them up and shoot. Whoever is left standing, wins." Miss Etta, to everyone's surprise, brought the Peacemaker out. "I'll make sure it's a fair fight. If anyone draws early, you lose. Got it?"

Everyone nodded in agreement. When everybody was in place, Miss Etta began the countdown.

"One...two..." Everybody was looking in their adversary's eyes. Colt and Dennis looked slightly scared. Alonzo and Josephine were calm, cool, and collected.

"THREE!!"

Four guns came up. Only two shots were fired. Dennis and Colt looked at each other in surprise. They looked down at their chests. Each had a hole in it with blood gushing out of the wounds. Alonzo and Josephine walked toward their marks with their guns still pointed.

Josephine walked up and took Colt's gun from his hand. "How does it feel to know a woman killed you?"

100

Colt tried a few times before sound came out of his mouth. "Who are you?"

"My name is Josephine Walker. You shot my father in the back while he was mending fences about six months ago. You shot him because he wouldn't sell you his prized race horse. Remember me now?"

Realization dawned in his eyes. "I...I wanted that horse real bad."

"Wanted it bad enough to kill for it?"

"I always get what I want."

"Do you now? Did you get the horse? No, you just killed an unarmed man. Now, you are dying. How does it feel?"

Colt collapsed to his knees. Josephine kneeled in front of him. "What do you want from me, woman?"

"I want to watch the life leave your body just like I watched the life leave my dad's."

"Bitch."

Josephine laughed. "I've been called worse. Alonzo, you got anything you need to say to this piece of shit before he dies?"

Dennis had already died. Alonzo had disarmed him and thrown the gun toward Miss Etta. He had crossed his hands over his chest and closed his eyes. "Yeah, I'll be right there."

Sheriff Jarrod Barker had heard the gun shots and ran towards them. Alonzo waved to him then kneeled down in front of Colt. Colt had closed his eyes. Alonzo slapped him a couple of times in the face. Colt opened his eyes and glared at Alonzo.

"What do you want?"

"Pretty much the same thing Josephine wanted. I want to watch the life leave your eyes. It shouldn't be too much longer the way the wound is bleeding. I'm sure you don't remember me either or maybe you do. You killed my dad while he was unloading a wagon of supplies. I would just like to know why. What did he do to you?"

"Where was he unloading the wagon?"

"Here."

"He was the owner of this store?" Colt frowned. "I don't remember. How long ago was it?"

"About ten years ago."

"Oh, God, that's when I was just starting out. I don't really know man. I've killed men that just looked at me the wrong way. I'm sorry. I just don't know." Colt slumped forward and held himself up with his hands.

Miss Etta had moved closer. Her voice quivered, "You mean you didn't even have a reason to shoot Charlie? You just shot him."

Colt raised his head up and looked at Miss Etta. "Do you know what was on the wagon?"

"Yeah, it was loaded with some guns and ammunition, saddles, bridles, saddle blankets, horse feed, that sort of thing."

"I remember. I was trying to get a new gun and some ammunition from him. He wouldn't give it to me. Said he needed to check off the list of what he had ordered first. I got mad and shot him."

"In the back." Alonzo and Josephine said at the same time. Colt groaned and slumped to the ground. Alonzo felt for a pulse and didn't find one. He looked at Josephine. "He's dead."

Josephine hugged Alonzo. "Thank God, it's over. I can finally go home now."

Alonzo frowned, "Home? You're going home?"

"Yes, I can go home now that Colt is dead. I miss my ranch. I miss my horses. I miss my house. I miss the workers. It's time."

Alonzo stood up and walked back to the store. Josephine looked bewildered.

"What did I say?" She asked Miss Etta.

Miss Etta patted her arm. "Just go talk to him."

Alonzo had gone in the back door. Josephine followed him. Smoke stung her eyes and nose as she entered the building. She went down the hall and found him standing in what was left of the front of the General Store. The fire had pretty much gutted it. There might be some things they could salvage but Josephine wasn't sure they would ever be able to rebuild.

"Alonzo, can we talk?"

"What's there to talk about? You are going home, end of story."

"No, not end of story. Alonzo, I have been on Colt's trail for six months. I'm tired. I need simplicity in my life. Most people think I am this tough lady, but I honestly just want someone to hold me and tell me it's going to be okay. I want to wake up in the morning beside the man I love. I want to cook, clean, ride my horses, and have a family."

Alonzo was hearing her words, but he wasn't sure she was meaning what he hoped she meant.

"I can do that."

"You can do what?"

"I can give you everything you need."

They stood and looked at each other. Josephine had fallen madly in love with Alonzo. She wasn't sure exactly when, but she knew she couldn't live without him. She was hoping she could talk him and Miss Etta into moving in with her after the wedding, of course.

"Alonzo are you saying what I think you are saying?"

Miss Etta had come into the store unnoticed by either one. She stood behind the burnt counter with her arms crossed.

Alonzo took Josephine's hands in his. "Josephine, this is going to sound stupid, but I fell in love with you the minute Jack fell in love with you. I have watched you grow stronger by the day trying to defend my mom and that only made me love you more. Josephine Walker, will you make me the happiest man in the world and marry me?"

Josephine smiled with tears in her eyes. "Alonzo Tucker, nothing would make me happier. But I have one condition."

"One condition?"

"Yep, you and your mom will move to my ranch with me. I love you both and can't imagine life without either of you."

Alonzo looked around him. "There's nothing left here for us. What do you think, Mom?"

Miss Etta came forward. "I say we pack up what we can salvage and take it with us. The sooner the better."

Alonzo walked up to his soon to be bride and captured her lips with his. Miss Etta looked around the burnt store one last time. "Charlie, we finally got him. You are going to have yourself a beautiful daughter-in-law. She's good for Alonzo. She'll keep him in line. Something neither one of us could do. I love you, Charlie."

Miss Etta walked into the storage room and packed what she could. She left Alonzo and Josephine kissing in the hollowed-out store front for the entire town to see.

I am 50 years old. I've lived in Western North Carolina all my life. I am a mother to one beautiful daughter. She is the light of my life. Even though she is 26 years old, she will always be my baby. I have always loved reading and spent most of my childhood in my room surrounded by the only thing that gave me comfort and that was books. I worked as a photographer for years and loved every minute of it. I have always loved taking pictures of anything and everything. I never thought of myself as writer until my wonderful daughter told me to give it a try. I do have a weird muse that helps me get into my writing and has helped me write three short stories so far. I have been working on a novel for about 10 years now but can't seem to finish it. Maybe one day...

.

Such Is the Nature of the Change

Stephen M. Coghlan

The massed choir was rough in tone and agonized in note, but their passion was pure and was reflected by the strength that the dying sang their final hymns. Saint Dismas wished to join them, but *The Rads* of the nuclear desert had long since rotted away his voice, until he could only speak in little more than a scratched whisper.

Such was the nature of *The Change*; the single day, the single hour, where two superpowers, one fading in glory but desperate to remain important, one rising, young, vibrant, with something to prove, had engaged each other in thermonuclear warfare. The exchange had lasted a single salvo each, but the results had altered the entire world. For most, it had been a brilliant moment, a bright flash, a blinding light, an evaporation of flesh and bone, a superheated cooking of blood.

Governments collapsed under the strain of the global fallout. Countries isolated themselves or hid deep inside the earth. Relief to the two powers who had fought the war was refused out of vengeance for the pain their conflict wrought. The lands and peoples were ostracized and ignored as their final curse killed those who had never been involved in the feud.

Salvation could only come from within.

Salvation could only be found from The Order of the Saints of the Apocalypse.

To them, *The Change* meant purpose, meant duty. It was a calling to a higher and nobler good. The Saints took it upon themselves to spread peace and tranquility through order and faith. It was their oath to bear the weight of the dead upon their shoulders, and to end the suffering of the dying survivors.

They offered relief, free from the sin of suicide.

Placing the barrel of his pistol against the first of the flock, Dismas listened as the final notes hung in the air, faded, extinguished. The Saint looked into the woman's glassy eyes, scorched blind by poison, saw the parchment-thin flesh. The blisters and sores, the lack of hair, the blood that came from her mouth and ears, and the smile of gratitude that broken her lips and twisted her warped flesh. She was not long for the world thanks to The Rads that still blew about, irradiated, toxic, which had signed her death warrant. It got into everything, food, water, air, and where it entered into flesh, the body rotted from the inside-out.

She muttered something through her toothless mouth, spoke nonsensical words to the higher power.

"Your confession," Dismas whispered, his own words whistled sharply, because his teeth were long absent too. The bombs' blasts had rattled him, shook him to the bone, but it was the lingering radiation that had rendered his mouth into swollen gums and twisted tongue, not the moment that had altered the world. "Has been heard."

The pop of the pistol was loud, but his ears were used to it, and partially deaf from the constant demand for his work.

The next to seek mercy walked around the fresh corpse, around the pile that had just grown by one, and the remaining choir began to sing again. More than a few lay within the pile of "The Blessed."

It was something that used to make Dismas feel that he was changing the lives of many, that he was helping the sick and afflicted find peace and serenity, but now it was only his duty, and he carried it out with the cold emotions of an automaton. Gone was the passion of his early years after The Change. In its place was only a sense of duty, a task to complete before he joined the rest of the flock as a burning corpse.

It took all morning to get to the end of those who awaited the Saint's "help," and the bodies burned slowly through lunch and through the afternoon, while Dismas preached to those who were not far enough gone and those that were too stubborn, words of respite, words of salvation, words of cause. By evening, the dead had transformed into dust that was cool enough to collect. The surviving villagers carted away the remains, but not before Dismas had done his duty and collected a jar of the faithful's ashes.

In time, the charred remains of mortal coils would find their way back to his order's headquarters, NuVatica, where the faithful dead would once more serve the living by being mixed into the propellant that fueled the Order's sacred bullets.

By night, he slept fitfully in the darkness of the artificial cave, a ruined basement. Thrice he awoke in a panic, and thrice he fought his way back to needed sleep, but every time he closed his eyes, the memories returned.

In the memories, he was Danny, a drunkard, a nuisance, a public menace. He stole, he lied, he cheated, and had it not been for his incarceration in a dingy cell in a precinct's basement, he would be nothing more than a radiated corpse.

It was his imprisonment that had preserved him when the bombs fell.

109

The concrete walls shook and trembled, his teeth rattled, dust fell from overhead, the plumbing ruptured, and clean water flooded the floor of his cell.

There he had languished, dying only of hunger, wilting from water that turned brackish, but he clung on. For amusement, he sang, he danced, he wrote using imaginary implements on walls rendered invisible in the blackness, he made enemies with chittering things that roamed in the darkness, that bit at him and fed on him, that gnawed not only on flesh, but on his sanity.

He had gone to war against the darkness. He had raved, he had challenged, he had stomped about in an effort to crush that which haunted him, and just when he threatened to descend into pure and unadulterated madness, salvation found him when the founders of his order, the brothers Peter and Paul, discovered his hole in their search for supplies.

To him, they were hosts of heaven, come to rescue him from his pit of hell. He offered himself to them, gave himself freely to his deliverers. When they dragged him into the dimness of the nuclear twilight, he screamed in pain at the light that was intense as a star to him, and blinded, he was guided to sanctuary.

There, the devout was given a new name, there, the devout was trained, there, Dismas earned the rights to wear the golden pins of mushroom-shaped devastation that all of his order bore on the collars of their dusters and greatcoats.

By morning, he was tired and exhausted.

Since no toxic rain fell from the sky, Dismas set out to reach the next town on his map. The parchment was composed of rough but accurate lines, lovingly etched by the scribes of NuVatica using what materials and knowledge they had on hand.

By midday, his walk had become a mindless march, so when he crested a hill that was little more than a pile of roughly scrubbed earth stubbled with patches of burnt grass and stunted trees, and spied the pack of wild dogs, he fell back behind the ridge in a combination of fright and self-preservation.

Some of the superpacks that had existed on the early days, fattened on the corpses of their late masters, had numbered in the hundreds. Thanks to hunting and lingering radiation, most had shrunk to two-score or less in number. The present group was not that large, but a dozen starving and maddened mutts were trouble, even for a well-armed Saint. Dismas only carried two pistols, partly for ceremony, partly for defense, and he only had enough ammo to perform his estimated duties plus a single, special round for himself. In the darkened world, one always had a way out. He had named his exit, Salvation.

Hoping to hide before the hounds picked up his scent, Dismas began moving parallel to the ridge. He kept his eyes on the pack, nervously fingering his weapons, so he did not notice the hole until it was too late.

Falling forward, he bashed his ribs against the concrete wall. Unable to catch himself, the Saint tumbled downwards, landing hard on the cement floor. If there had not been a fine layer of garbage to help cushion his fall, he would have broken his ankle or snapped his wrist, yet he did not escape unharmed. His leg felt pierced with pain, and he barked his forearms badly enough to bleed. He landed roughly on his back, but rolled and protected his head from worse.

He collected his breath, only for his conscious mind to realize that he was, once more, below ground. He tried to fight back the panic as he scrabbled his way to the nearest wall, fought to control his breathing as he found the ladder, and only once he had some semblance of control, only once he had fought back the fright, collected his beaten and faded Stetson, and wiped the tears from his face, did he begin to explore the darkened abyss.

At first there was nothing useful, the garbage and litter that had broken his fall was composed of discarded food containers and used latrine bags, but just before he was about to abandon the site and return to the perilous but open sky, he chanced upon a note.

Geoff:

It read in harried scrawl, visible even in the dim light.

We can't wait anymore. We used up the last of the water today filling the bottles, so we're going with plan C. We're going to head due South and hope that we find something.

Love you. Please hurry and find us.

The page was unyellowed, the ink, clear. It was tacked to the ladder itself, and in such pristine condition that it could only have been written within the last few days. More importantly, it was evidence of a Puritan, a survivor who had escaped the moment of Change, who had survived the ravages that had followed, hidden away from the deaths and plagues that haunted other survivors.

A prayer of hope escaped Dismas' swollen mouth. His order had a duty towards Puritans, a need to escort them to the one remaining haven for the untainted of the flock, Eden, a special location where The Order hoped to rebuild humanity free from the residual effects of ionizing radiation.

Pocketing the note, so that others would not find it, Dismas returned to the overworld and began his new mission.

The first sign that he was on the right track, other than the occasional footprint, was when he found the desiccated and desecrated mummy of a middle-aged woman. Her body was a stripped and shriveled husk, which meant that she, and most likely her entire party, had been waylaid.

Safe water was scarce among the wastes. Blood robbing, harvesting others for their fluids, had become a common profession. The healthy were the optimum prey, as their uncontaminated fluids fetched prime purchase on the black market.

There was no skin pulled tight over the corpse, which indicated that the blood robber had not worked alone. Flesh Takers were another danger of the wastes, but the garments they produced were the best that one could own against the rigors of the land.

There was nothing else, save a single discarded plastic bottle, crushed flat. The captors had obviously celebrated their claim.

Inspecting his map, Dismas turned for the closest trading village, and, straightening his collar, he continued his trek.

Darkness had coated the land by the time he saw the glowing fires of dustbins and torches, but despite the late hour, he still heard the sounds of 'civilization.' Market towns never truly slept. Garish music on pre-Change antiques and modern songs made using recycled materials permeated the air. Old billboards, their original messages long-since faded and painted over in poorly spelled attractions, swung on noisy chains or clacked against tent poles and rickety shacks.

Dreenks read one. *Weponz* read another. *Fude here, luv schak, Nik-naks*

Dismas did not search by store, but by occupants. He found them at a bar that served cheap moonshine and expensive water, celebrating still. The Blood Robber was unmistakable, the odor of death that permeated from him was a dead giveaway and he wore the tell-tale equipment of large metal and glass cylinders, strapped to his back. The Flesh Taker was more subtle, but her dark clothes shone with a thin coating of once-human fat and her belt of knives and vicious hooks clinked as she raised another glass into the air.

"To untainted rind!" She cried.

"Skin is only the casing that keeps the inside juicy." Laughed the Blood Robber as he toasted in return.

Adjusting his uniform, the Saint made sure that the two mushroom-cloud pins were more than visible before he approached, pulled up a chair, and sat across from the celebrants. "Excuse me." He whispered through his damaged throat, removing his hat to expose his scarred and pocked scalp.

"Father." The Blood Runner smiled and raised his glass again.

"I'm following puritans." Dismas got straight to the point. "Did you drain them all?"

"Just the mother." The Flesh Taker bragged. "We sold the daughters for a very good price."

"I am glad that you spared them." The Saint said with a sigh. "To whom did you sell?"

"Client confidentiality." The Blood Robber chuckled.

From the folds of his clothes, Dismas produced a small sack of pop-can tabs and placed them on the table. They were one of the more recognized currencies, and he hoped the amount was sufficient, but when the Flesh Taker weighed it by juggling it a few times, she threw it back down on the table with a grimace of disgust.

"Tempting." The Flesh Taker admitted. "But not worth the cost to my own hide."

"Our client has a reputation for silencing those who blab." The Blood Robber poured himself another drink.

Reaching to his belt, Dismas carefully placed six bullets down upon the table. "Final offer." He whispered.

"You don't get it, you moron!" The Blood Robber roared. "You can't bribe us! We're dead if we speak!"

He made as if to stand, and at that moment, Dismas had enough. His order preached peace, but it also preached obedience, and, where necessary, righteous anger.

"I will offer once more." Dismas whispered, narrowing his eyes.

The Blood Robber stood in anger.

Drawing his pistol, Dismas held down on the trigger while his free hand slapped the hammer thrice. The first bullet carved through his target's chest, shattering the large glass vial that the Blood Robber wore on his back. The second through his throat, the third, emptied the head of mind and brain.

He swung the barrel towards the Flesh Taker, but the woman had already knelt and began to pull the valuables from her companion's corpse. From another stall, a meat merchant came to offer a price on the freshly dead.

"They were sold to a brothel." The Flesh Taker answered as she stood, her eyes wet with tears as the butcher paid for the flesh. "Their caravan was heading west. We sold them only an hour ago. I doubt they've even left town."

With a nod of thanks, Dismas sipped at an unfinished shot of moonshine. Leaving the bag of tabs as a thank you and apology, The Saint doffed his cap, adjusted his robes, and headed to the caravans.

What he saw was not encouraging. A hobbled accountant rode about on a palanquin, carried on the backs of permanently hunched slaves while all were shielded by heavily armed guards.

Dismas made sure he was presentable as he approached the head merchant,

"Can I help you, father?" The leader of the caravan asked, digging one thick finger, unwieldy and slow with fat, into his nasal cavity. His voice was further muffled by the multiple chins that choked his throat.

"I am looking for a mule." Dismas responded in his hoarse whisper.

The merchant laughed, the rolls of excess flesh jiggling in the process. "Am I to assume for standard hauling purposes?" The tone was mocking, already preparing for a negative, but Dismas did not responded in kind.

The laugh was not unexpected. Clapping his profuse fingers together, the merchant summoned a small collection of youthful 'merchandise'. "Peruse as you will, father. These are similar to others that I have sold to your order." The seller of souls winked in amusement.

115

Bile rose in Dismas' throat, but he did not say much as he feigned interest, walking up and down the ranks. He hoped that the merchant was lying about his companions, prayed that the rich waste of skin was goading him.

Not one was a Puritan.

"I am hoping for something less, tainted." The Saint sighed when he came to the end of the line.

"I don't think you have enough money in your order for that." The Merchant hissed, his small eyes narrowed. "These alone are worth their weight, and your companions have never complained about my quality."

"Of course, I did not mean to offend." Dismas lied. "Allow me to 'sleep' on it. The one that comes to mind, I will return to buy."

"Do not delay, father." The merchant advised. "We leave in the morning."

Nodding, Dismas began to walk away. "I understand." He chuckled, waving a hand casually, but his thoughts did not match his outer serenity. He wished little more than to rid the unrighteous from the world, but he knew an attack against such a heavily armed group who were entrenched in the safety of a town, was tantamount to suicide.

There was more than one route to salvation. He found the tent he wanted beside the meat merchant who had purchased the blood robber's corpse. A new sign hung over their tables that advertised "Fresh Flesh."

Ignoring the wet mouths and lust filled eyes of the consumers, Dismas pulled his hat low over his head and entered the small bivouac. Above the entrance a single dot, and three almost triangles, equally spaced, were painted on a placard. It was a symbol of his faith.

The lone occupant smiled in greeting. Raising himself from his bunk, The Minister swung his clubbed feet to the woven mats. He was large in head, small in body, a boy, walking about on a cane.

"Praise be for The Change."

"Praise be." Dismas answered, dusted his hat with his hands, and then announced his reason for entrance. "I need a louder voice."

"For what purpose, brother?"

"To save some Puritans."

"Ah, more breeders." The boy laughed and snickered. "More cattle for our leaders' stock."

Pushing the carpets aside, The Minister exposed a buried trunk, which, when opened, revealed a small collection of weapons and armor. Making his selection, Dismas began to arm himself while his companion sat back upon his bunk and chortled.

"The Puritans will be well kept, the lucky ones will be well fed, then they will be well bred." It was a song, filled with disdain, marked by The Minister's heavy feet, thumping against the floor.

"It is not proper for a Minister to mock our Eden, so." Dismas cautioned.

"Why not, you ever served there?" The youth snickered. "Among the captives they shall be, forced to live, eternally impaled by our great leaders."

"I would silence your mouth, heathen." The Saint growled, strapping a shirt of leather and plate over himself."

"Why, do you still believe in the piousness of your cause? If so, you are far too blind. I have seen the truth here, when other Saints bring in their charges to this tent and take them as their own. I have seen the breeding Puritans, and I have known what happens when our great leaders visit them for evenings of 'lessons and scripture.'"

A bandolier of shells were added, and Dismas reared menacingly to his full height, but the youth ignored him.

"I have known, first hand, the touch of their divinity. I felt it, night after night until I became too old for their sickly tastes, and I was cast here, to hide my shame." The youth was fire in his own. "Even my father and my uncle, your great hosts, have left their remnants of "communion" inside of me."

That gave Dismas pause, and he looked back at the youth, a child, no older than a dozen years, cast to a far outpost, and he wondered at the validity of his words.

"As long as humanity exists, they will fabricate Gods, so that the strong may control the weak. Our deity was crafted in nuclear annihilation. All you serve, in the end, is the greed of man and power and wealth. All the good you have done is fed falsities to the masses, and now, you lead two more innocents to the corruption of the word."

Sitting up, the hunched Minister smiled knowingly. "If the truth I speak upsets you, then finish this conversation. Remove me, and live on the power we have given you to abuse."

Rage at the attack of his faith threatened to doom The Minister, but Dismas held back his fury with effort, and only once the urge to bring righteous justice upon the youth's skull had passed, did he close the trunk and retire to the far edge of the tent, to wait until dawn.

The caravan did not leave until almost noon. It was clear, once they began to move, that they did not plan to deviate from their one heading, so neither did Dismas. Field glasses let the Saint examine the columns. They hurried to make up for lost time, and all day, those who were chained, walked across the hot and dusty scrubland. The guards were many, and those not actively scanning for dangers, instead scanned their numbers for weaklings or those who stumbled.

By evening, his prayers that the Puritans were there was answered. Two girls, maybe a decade and a half in age, each, were escorted from a covered wagon, to a small copse of bushes for only a few moments. Their clothes were tattered and faded from age and wear, but not stained by the environment. Their frames were skinny and rakish from years of rations, but they did not appear malnourished.

Satisfied, the Saint hurried to prepare his ambush, and without flaw, they walked directly into it just before midnight. Old claymores, discovered by one of Dismas' spiritual brothers, burst directly into the faces of the front guards while buried sticks of explosives detonated moments later at the rear, blocking both advance and retreat.

In the chaos of the opening explosion, Dismas run up a dry riverbed, having chosen it for its cover. The wagon's guards noticed him too late, and Dismas' shot caught the first guard above the heart. The other guard fired off a pistol of his own, but he was nervous, and his shot went wide. Dismas' return did not.

Another explosion near the front, another delayed fuse, kept his opponents confused and at bay. It was little more than packages of firecrackers now. They were unstable, leaky things, but they only had to keep the enemy scattered, and for that they were more than sufficient.

A knife cut into the thick canvas of the wagon. Peeking through the hole, Dismas shot a third guard who wandered back and forth, crossbow at the ready. The screams of the witnesses were subdued by the ringing in his ears.

Each prisoner was flawless or beautiful in their own rights. They were the special, the harem slaves, the ones sold for pleasure or display. It wasn't hard to find the Puritans. They had not yet been cleaned for auction, they still had all their hair, and their skins were burnt by the harsh suns already since they had been raised belowground, and had not built up a natural resistance or tan.

Although others looked at him with hope of freedom in their eyes, he ignored the rest. The two girls sat nervously, holding each other, and they winced in worry as he approached them, but his knife made short work of their bonds.

"Move!" Dismas whispered harshly, pulling his charges along with him.

Once more in the night, it became obvious that the chaos of his plan was beginning to fade. A ball of lead flattened itself against his armor, flooring him and breaking a rib in the process. Where shock stopped his mind, training took over. The Saint's pistol barked thrice, killing the woman who had shot him.

To the Puritans' credit, neither girl had stopped to check on him, but instead ran into the cover of the riverbed. Dragging himself to his feet, Dismas hurried after.

The sounds of their struggle became audible only when he was almost on top of them. Another guard had sought shelter within the cover that had concealed Dismas' advance. The brute held one girl by the arm while her sister beat on the massive man's back to no avail.

Without hesitation, Dismas emptied the rest of his pistol into the brute's side, and at that range, all four remaining rounds found lodging in flesh.

The big one collapsed.

The Puritan that the brute had been handling was in poor shape. She had been smacked hard across the face, and the blow had stunned her. Ripping a piece of his tunic free, Dismas bent to administer a basic field dressing when her eyes grew large.

Something ripped through his back, gouged his intestine, and exited out his gut. There was no immediate pain, and his body numbed as Dismas was lifted into the air by whatever had impaled him, before being flung aside.

Landing hard, he tried to stand, tried to fight back, but his body refused to respond properly. When he got his hands underneath him a kick to the wound sent him screaming as much as his damaged throat could manage.

A second kick knocked some of his weapons free and caused him to roll to the side. One more kick, and then Dismas was picked up and smashed bodily against a wall of stone and pebble.

Coughing blood, the wounded beast whom Dismas had taken for dead, leaned in, snarling ferally, desperate to bring pain to the one who had harmed him.

The boom of the shotgun announced the blast that tore a hole in the beast man's side. The big one released Dismas, stumbled, and then the big gun barked again, and the monster man fell, but did not die. When he tried to stand again, Dismas knew he had to end it.

Before the Saint began a search for a weapon, a pistol was slapped into his fingers. Planting the barrel against his opponent's forehead, the Saint made sure he and his foe met eyes.

Then he pulled the trigger, and the beast man was felled.

Collapsing on top of his foe, Dismas tried to gather the will to stand, but the pain and weakness from the blow leached throughout, draining him of any further capability.

"Help him." The girl who had fired the shotgun into the brute yelled, but the Saint felt both arms being pulled, and he noticed that the two girls he had hoped to rescue, were instead, rescuing him.

Together, they limped to a rock that overhang the edge of the riverbed. There was a small space beneath it, accessible only by crawling. Falling to his hands and knees, the wounded Saint pulled himself inside only to fall down into the blackened hole, where it was big enough to almost stand. Had it not been for the visibility at his eye level, he would have immediately left again, screaming, fleeing into the night.

The woman with the shotgun stood guard, nervously, shakily, uncertain, while her sister recovered the spilled weapons and hat that Dismas had dropped when the Brute had beaten him. By the time they wormed their way into the hole beside their rescuer, the small cave smelled of burned flesh and lit propellant. Against the far wall, the Saint languished in shock. The wound in his stomach was cauterized thanks to the powder of his bullets and a smoking match.

Raising one shaking hand, Dismas aimed a pistol at the opening by steadying it on a rock, and together, they waited for what was to come.

"Marisa, wait." Dismas cautioned.

The older twin hesitated, she was on all fours, her face inches from the top of a puddle.

Taking a small vial of dye, the Saint tossed a drop into the water, and it sparkled as if it was a bright star on a pitch night as whatever was in the water reacted dangerously with the potion that had been added to it.

Sighing, Maria checked the level of her flask. It was almost empty, and she had been the most conservative on their journey.

Drawing his knife, Dismas leaned against a small plant, and after feeling the few leaves that attempted to grow, cut one in twain. He handed the portions to the two girls, and they sucked on the moisture, greedily.

They had been on the run together for over two weeks.

Thanks to the map, they had found a healer who had performed rudimentary surgery on the Saint. It was not pretty, nor precise, but it left him able to walk, and although he still bled, the blood loss was slowed to something that he could endure.

Thanks to the weapons they had preserved, they had fought off wild dogs, bounty hunters, and more than one tracking member from the caravan.

Thanks to the Saint's survival, the girls had begun to adapt to the burned and parched wastes. Their cushioned life in the shelter had left them with great theoretical knowledge, but they had no experience in the harshness of the modern world. Their minds were pliable, however, and their ability to accept the new reality was a blessing.

They had not forgotten what had happened to their mother when the Flesh Taker had done her work, and the Blood Robber's clinical precision had transformed the corpse to a husk. They understood too, that if they had not been saved, what would have awaited them at the hands of their masters.

Marisa was the older twin, ambitious, determined, course of tongue and free of speech. A single chip in a front tooth was the only way Dismas told the two girls apart, once the swelling from the Brute's beatings had descended. She had earned the dentin difference by apparently leaping from furniture, while attempting to stave off the boredom of living isolated, underground.

Maria was quieter and more polite, but she was no less intelligent, and no less brave. She had learned fast and had shown a natural talent with the pistol, and her determination to remain 'pure' had let her kill, coldly, when faced with only negative alternatives.

His two charges had grown on him, and had become special to the Saint. They had transformed from a duty, a mission, into friends and allies, something that was a precious commodity in the scorched lands.

That was why Dismas was torn in his task. He had to know if the twisted Minister of the tent had spoken the truth. He had to know if he was saving and preserving purity or merely placing it into the hands of another corrupter.

"Don't worry about our water supplies. We're almost there." Dismas whispered, and guided his too charges up the hill. When they reached the crest, the scent of vegetation was almost overpowering.

Eden was laid out before them. Acres of lush, green vegetation fought back, resisted against the rot of the wastes, and even, began to win. The sight made his two charges stare in awe. They had lived within steel and concrete, only to emerge to dust and death.

Falling to his knees, Dismas smiled.

"It's going to be, alright." He whispered, raising one pistol into the air, he coughed, and blood flecked his chin. Digging with his free hand, he found a stone, and when he fired his pistol, he jammed the rock against his wound, ruining the coverings and aggravating the injury.

Collapsing to the soft green grass, he watched and listened as cries of attention were raised. A smile creased his broken face, and as he disappeared into darkness, he let himself feel glad that he had accomplished the first part of his mission.

He had not felt clean sheets for months, and the feeling was indescribable in its luxury.

Opening his eyes, Saint Dismas looked about, and made sure he was alone.

He had spent the last few hours feigning sleep, when in reality, he had been preparing for war. Only a few hours ago, he had been awakened with the news that the surgery was done, and that he would live to fight another day. While the words were welcome, who informed him, was not.

Why had the heads of his order, the brothers, Peter and Paul, been at Eden, and not at their posts in NuVatica?

Dismas feared he knew the answer.

The steel floor of the lab leached heat from his toes, but the callouses of his feet protected him from chills. He was naked, save for the bandages, and the chain about his neck, which held Salvation in its small sling.

The sterility of the medical wing was alien to him. Dismas had never set foot within such cleanliness once since The Change. He was a Saint, his duty was the field, and that was where he belonged.

It was not quiet in the halls. Ophanim hurried about. They were the wheels, the gears, the troops that kept the order moving. They were the orderlies, they were the mechanics, the gun smiths, and the accountants.

It was not easy to avoid them, even in the night. The medical wing was filled with the sounds of crying infants, medical equipment, and muted conversations.

Dismas' time in the wastes had taught him how to hide, how to move quietly despite the pain of his injuries. A set of stairs finally led to a different wing, an undiscovered section, the quarters of the Puritans, and despite the warnings, the Saint was still shocked to see his belief in the system that had saved him so violated.

The first quarters he opened exposed the truth in its naked and horrendous details. The woman was chained to the bed, and her eyes were of the hollow and defeated. A snarling and brutish man stood between her legs, naked, prepared. Dismas knew of him by reputation alone, but it was enough. He was a merchant of melted metals, one of the richest and most profitable and therefor powerful people of the wastes.

He was not pure, he was twisted and sickly from The Rads, despite being large in shoulder and thick of arm.

The anger that filled Dismas gave him strength. Moving swiftly, he smashed one fist into the wealthy one's face, stunning him. It was easy from there to position himself behind the corrupted one. The move was simple, fast, properly executed, and the wealthy one's neck gave with a crack.

It was that noise that brought life back to the chained woman, and she looked at Dismas with a combination of hope and fear. Realizing that his robes had become disturbed, the Saint felt embarrassed and hid his shame before he searched for a method to free the woman who had suffered.

The next room held two men, also restrained, and in another, costumed captives whined and hid from the opening of the door.

There was no emotion to describe the betrayal and rage that coursed through his system. The violation of his faith consumed him. Gone was the love of his fellows. He had honored a system, and he felt himself as the lone pious herald. It was his duty to purge the corrupted. It was his duty to purify, to set the others straight. He was the flood, he the rain of fire and brimstone. He the flames of bitumen.

When he encountered a guard who had known and accepted his role as a guardian of Gomorrah, Dismas stole upon him and delivered justice. His guns, his clothes, his blade, became property of the Saint, became tools of vengeance.

Any that claimed to be of his order yet served such an ignoble duty were dealt with. A throat was slashed, another disemboweled, and another, brutally interrogated before being sent to final judgement.

Dismas had his destination.

The door beyond was both his hope and his dread. He hesitated, worried that he would open the portal only to see the two young girls violated, ruined. He prayed to any God that would listen that their purity was still intact, that he had not brought them only to ruin their souls.

A pipe landed upon his shoulder, and had he not been dressed in thick clothes from his once associates, it would have hurt him further. Instead of raising his pistols, Dismas did something he had not thought he could ever do again. He laughed.

It was a laugh caused by relief and pride. Marisa had tried to attack him with a portion of headboard she and Maria had broken from the great bed, while her sister wielded a large chunk of wood as a shield. They were cleaned, dressed in gossamer garments, but they both stood, prepared to fight.

The ragged cough told the girls who their visitor was, and when he dropped two coats and the weapons he had appropriated from his once allies, they understood that he was still their guardian.

"Let's go." He whispered ecstatically.

They stepped into the hall, only to see two "Saints" marching in. They were unmistakable to Dismas, and he stepped in front of the twins to face the men who had once given him a reason to live.

"Blessed be!" Paul yelled, ecstatically, one hand held out in greeting, the other, hidden within his jacket. "We had heard that Eden was under attack. Thank you for protecting them."

Peter smiled a toothless grin, having also been rotted from his time in the field. "You have done well, Brother." His voice had a tremble of lust. It was naked, unashamed. Both hands were within his clothes, but there was no mistaking the barrel that shifted. "They will help us rebuild."

The two girls moved closer to their guardian, instinctively seeking comfort from their guide and protector.

"Thank you for bringing them to safety." Paul continued. "We understand if you are confused-"

"I have never been more certain of things in my life." Dismas snarled. The pain of the lies forced his hand, and he raised to fire, but Peter and Paul had been prepared. The booms of four guns echoed throughout the halls. At that close range, Paul's Magnum demolished the appropriated armor about Dismas' stomach, but in return, Dismas' shot caught Paul on the edge of the chin, tumbled into his throat, and punched a messy and ragged hole through his spine.

Peter's round caught Dismas on the shoulder, but Dismas' round was just over his former teacher's heart, and in passing, shattered rib, and sent bone fragments deep within the vital organ. They both stumbled.

Behind Dismas, two more guns spoke, and the bodies of his once saviors were holed again.

Gasping, Dismas tried to find his feet, but the shots he had received had done their worst. Blood poured from his body in quantities too great to stop.

It took effort, but he removed his gun belts and tossed them to the feet of the girls.

"Go." He whispered. "Please."

The twins bent to retrieve the weapons, when, with a roar, they were attacked by a man thought dead. Peter charged, blood leaking down his chest, crimson fluid, frothing from his mouth. Strength fueled him, and Dismas arrested his mentor. They bounced into the wall, and Peter tried to fire again, but the round traveled down the hall. A punch, an attempt at a bludgeon, and another shot buried itself above the heads of the two girls. An elbow, a kick, another shot into the ceiling.

With screams of their own, Marisa and Maria caught Peter's legs, and pulled them from underneath. Dismas fell on top, but his advantage was lost when iron fingers wrapped around his neck.

A new round sparked down the hall. More guards had arrived, and the two girls broke from the fight of the wounded in order to return fire.

"Burn, Heretic!" Peter ragged.

Desperate, Dismas pushed his thumbs into his former leader's eyes. Screaming, Peter released his protégé.

Peter's gun lay near. Taking it in his shaking hands, he pulled the trigger, but it landed on an empty chamber. Cracking the cylinder, he saw the gun was empty.

There was only one bullet close enough to help.

Salvation

Removing the special bullet, carved with the mushroom shaped blast of his former faith, Dismas loaded it into the chamber. His hands were shaking, his movements, unsteady. As he worked, he heard the girls yelling his name, saw the two of them reloading, saw them using cover.

Pulling back on the hammer, Dismas aimed high, and the round passed through the bridge of Peter's nose and traveled into his mind, scrambling brain tissue into liquid before exiting in an explosion of thought.

Falling prone, Dismas spied Paul's magnum and belt of ammunition. He fired, his aim steadied on the corpse of the gun's former owner. Each shot found a mark, each shot, silenced another whom Dismas once called, brother.

Then, there was momentary silence.

"Please." Dismas begged his charges. "Go, while there is still time."

He felt lips upon his rotten flesh. Each cheek, blessed by his charges touch.

"Are you sure?" The eldest asked.

"We can get you to a doctor." The youngest added.

Their Saint looked sadly at them. He wished nothing more, but he already felt his life fleeing from his body.

New bullets passed overhead, and Dismas returned fire. By the time he had need to reload, the twins were gone.

Opening his mouth, he began to sing a hymn, his requiem, as he prepared to martyr himself for his belief, for his hope that he made a difference. The two girls would be his act of salvation, not his bullet. Thanks to him, they would survive, they could fight, they could scavenge. Thanks to him, they would live free lives, and in those last moments, with the realization that he had done something right, had truly practiced the salvation he had preached, he too, was alive.

Stephen Coghlan is an ever-expanding multi-genre author who writes from the Maple Syrup region of Canada's National Capital. Feel free to check out his website at http://scoghlan.com, or find him on Facebook and Twitter as @WordsBySC, where you can discover where his written wonders will take you next.

ABSOLUTION

PATRICK WINTERS

The sun was hot. The day had been long. The ride had been longer. Still, the man spurred his horse on, huffing and puffing and grunting through the expansive country that sat beneath a godless sky. The Texas border now lay an untold number of sprawling miles behind him, along with a fair portion of the Chihuahuan Desert. The remainder of the arid land and all the rest of the state lay before him, waiting for his and other nomads' arrival. At mid-day, the sun sat straight overhead, bathing the landscape in yellow-gold light that shone with a greater blaze than even Holy Fire could burn. Waves of heat wove and shimmered with scintillating ebbs and flows in the middle distance and would not part nor abate for any traveler. They rolled shifted and flowed on, always near but ever out of reach.

Brush sprouted forth from the dusty, dry earth in hues of green and red. They grew with hesitant life, their branches and twigs reaching up to the heavens like worshipers before the pulpit. Still, others were dead or well on their way to being dead. Bare and withered and colored in odd grays. Their roots did not delve deeply enough or spread far enough to drink from whatever water lay within the secretive earth underfoot, and they were

131

dying for it. A stiff breeze could topple them or uproot them or disintegrate them, to be blown into so much dust upon the zephyr, if only such a wind could be mustered on this desolate day. But the land did not breathe; it let the sweltering heat have its way with whom or whatever dared to trek its many miles.

He dared, and the horse he rode followed under his compulsion and his reigns. He lifted a crud-covered hand to his stubble-covered cheek, scratching at a heated itch that had become persistent. The skin of his cracked fingertips swabbed at the sweat slipping down from his brow, stirring the dirt that had gathered on his face and turning it into a thin muck on his cheek. He was in need of water, himself, and would dig down into the earth and take what little there was from the brush and weeds, if only he knew where to dig. His canteen had dropped its last little drop hours before, and his limbs felt as weak and brittle as those of the bushes and brush about him. The tedium of travel had long-since set in and he'd made his way further and further through the country like a pilgrim who'd long since forgotten the site they sought.

Miles passed. Hours passed. He came upon no towns. No life.

More miles passed.

Turning his eyes to the skies, the man saw dark shapes whirling and twirling about against the deep blue heavens. Though at first indefinite, their feathered forms came into better view as he drew closer to where they hovered. Three large vultures swooped and spun in slow, broad circles in the sky, straight ahead. Their long, full-dark wings stretched out like those of fallen angels as they gradually lowered themselves down to the ground, bit by bit. The man saw them touch down and ruffle their wings in anticipation. They hobbled about an indistinct form, laid sprawled on the dusty earth. He heard them chitter and squawk to each other. One gave a shrill screech to offend the ears, and which came back to them as it echoed through the vast country.

The man spurred his horse to move quicker.

Their approach caused the vultures to squawk and call and bare their dark beaks in a scavenger's disdain, and their wings to flutter up and out in warning. They danced about the body of the dead man they had found and intended to have as a meal. One advanced ahead of the others; it clacked and snapped its beak as it carried on, intent on defending the spoiling morsel. The man pulled out his revolver, thumbed the hammer, and sent an aimless shot at the ground, before the boldest of the three; it rang out in the stillness and set a puff of dust into the air, the bullet tearing into the earth.

The scavenger leapt back a pace and a feather or two flew in its flustered retreat. The three gave flight, still calling out in anger. Their shadows grew large and swooped along the ground as they began circling in the air once more. They waited.

The man pulled his horse to a stop beside the body. Its dead smell had since wafted to his nose, and it was made all the mightier and more pungent as the meat cooked and rotted under that blazing sun above. The nag was not so perturbed by the acrid stench; it turned its head to the dead man, sniffing at his still and bloodied chest. It gave a quick lick at the great red stain that had soaked across the man's raggedy vest, spreading forth from a bullet-hole that had torn through it, the shirt under it, and on into his meat and bone beneath. Not caring for the taste after all, the nag turned its head to face forward once more, looking dully at a gray bush just ahead.

The man stared down at the body, looking it over.

Opened, sightless eyes sat beneath circle-rimmed bifocals; their death-stare was hidden beneath the lenses—one cracked, both dirtied and opaque, dust stuck fast to the glass. They may have stared straight up at the man or up towards the cloudless and godless firmament; the man couldn't tell which, for sure. A tattered brown bowler hat lay tilted beside the body's still head, the man's locks of brown-blonde hair fanned out and stretching towards it as though to reclaim it, put it on his scalp, and bring life back to his limbs, in turn. Trickles of dull red had leaked out of the corners of the man's mouth, like sacred wine spilling forth from the lip of an overturned communion cup. It had long since dried under the heat of the sun. It stuck to the man's stubble-studded skin in cracked and darkened rivulets that were slowly disappearing under the layers of dust gathering on the corpse; the skin and clothing looked yellow from all the grime coating it. With the passing of another day, the body may end up completely covered in dirt, to be mistaken for a mound of sand in the vast expanse that lay all around. If the vultures had their fill of his meaty shell and left nothing but bones, they would bleach under the sun before getting lost within the earth. A wanderer could trip across them thinking he'd snagged his boot on a root when it was in fact a rib-cage. And they would walk on, none the wiser.

The man saw no canteen on the body. No hint of a pouch or wallet beneath his clothing, either. Nothing of worth; not much reason to stay and sit around gawking.

He set his horse back to stepping along and left the vultures to their fetid find. They called out in vicious victory as they came back down to feed. He did not turn around to see them do so.

More miles passed.

The sun kept creeping along down the sky, each fraction of an inch matching a league traveled. The peaks of the Sierra Madre to the west grew more and more distant as the man headed east, their incredible mass just a series of subtle protuberances set into the vast and far horizons that mortal eyes could hardly fathom in full. He did not turn to look upon them again but kept moving forward, gradually putting the sun to his back, in turn.

After innumerable hours, and when the sun had nearly completed its descent beyond the western edge of the earth, the faint sight of buildings and lodging came into the man's sights. A town lay before him. He urged his horse to move at a swifter pace.

When he reached the outskirts of the town, the first edifice he came upon was a general store. On its broad side hung a large, wide sign that was meant to give the name of the town in austere and welcoming lettering. Whatever had been writ upon it, though, had faded with the passage of time and the unforgiving will of the elements. It had been sand-blasted and rain-pelted and worn down to where its paint was a muddled blur, the name left indescribable. A fresh, wet stain dripped down its bottom corner, where an irate drunkard had launched a not-so downed bottle of something. Whether in outright anger, defiance, or simple displeasure and orneriness, the sign had been defaced recently, and the name upon it left to more damage.

The man rode further into town and down along its main street, coming across a smithy's shack, a meager bank, and a decrepit haberdashery. No saloon yet. No place to slake his thirst and wipe his brow of the sweat that had persisted to sop his skin.

He had passed only a meandering towns-person or two when he heard the sound of mournful crying and sobbing.

As he turned his horse down a corner, he saw what must have been the bulk of the town standing in a wide street-way. They stood to either side of the way, close to the ramshackle buildings, heads mostly bowed as a line of others moved slowly along the street and towards his direction. At the lead of the procession were four men dressed in their Sunday best, and who carried a rather small pine box between them. They moved silently and in time, the burden they hefted not weighty enough to draw any huffs of exertion. A line of a dozen or so others walked a few paces behind them, many in black, the rest in the cleanest and most representable clothing they could afford, and more was the pity.

135

The cries the man had heard came from a young, plain woman among the people, and who was lead on by two other plain, older women.

He caught a glance of what looked to be the front of a saloon down the way. His thirst rose but the funeral procession barred the way to the establishment. He would wait until it had passed.

He inched his horse along and to the side, stopping it at the end of the nearest gathering of mourners. None offered up even the slightest of greetings to the stranger among them, though several looked his way with a tinge of curiosity, breaking the veneer of their woeful looks. Some, in truth, did not even look woeful—they simply stood amidst the ones that did, to complete the practice of respect and farewell, and to keep those chains of community as tightly linked as their sentiments could muster. No tears or sobs or sighs came from them, and they looked from the casket to their feet, waiting as patiently as the man now did.

The men bearing the tiny casket passed before him, their eyes to the ground, keeping their slow pace in tact with every step. As the young crying woman passed, she burst out into a wail that would have rung through the plain, if there had been a wind to carry it. One of the elderly women beside her gave a lurch at the noise, and the other moved closer to the mourning woman.

The old woman set her arm about the younger in both caring comfort and knowing authority. "He's gone to Heaven, child. A far better place than here."

The girl-woman nodded, but her tears kept falling.

"This world makes men out of children. Hard, harsh men. Your boy left us with virtue."

Anything else said between them was lost to the man's ears as they trudged on by, off towards the outskirts of town, where a paltry cemetery lay. Its tombstones stuck up from the earth in odd angles like teeth in a scamp's mouth. A lowly looking wooden fence bordered the resting spots, where another was on its way to search for rest, if there were any to be found.

The crowd of mourners, well-wishers, and onlookers dispersed, and the man dispersed with them. Some followed the procession on to the cemetery —most went about their own business, whatever that may have been. All were silent as they went along.

The man continued towards the saloon, where he tied up his horse before stepping into the establishment.

The room was dimly lit by dwindling candles set all over, and it smelled musky. A bartender with a face as cracked and rough as basalt moved with slow disinterest towards a table of young patrons. He caught sight of the man and made a shrug as though to sit wherever his hindquarters cared to roost, and that he'd be right with him.

The man took a stool at the bar-top, its wooden face covered by knife nicks and sawdust. He waited for the bartender to tend to him, staring at the blank wall across from the counter. When the bartender trudged back over, he asked: "What'll ya have?"

The man answered: "Water first. Whiskey second." He pulled out a pouch of coin from within his vest and set it on the countertop, to get the bartender moving a bit more quickly. The old man did just that, turning to his inventory and glasses.

Someone burst through the doors with a harsh call that grabbed the man's attention. He turned to see a portly gent with a mustache as long as Tennessee and a broad hat on his head. The man recognized him from the crowd about the funeral procession. He'd been one of those who hadn't cried.

"Adam! Whiskey, as always!"

The bartender answered the call with a simple grunt, and the gent moved over to sit by a lone fellow sitting at the other end of the bar-top. The mustached man addressed him as Stephen, and the other gave a nod.

"Went to the burying, did you?" the fellow named Stephen asked the mustached man.

"Oh no," the gent said. "I don't dare get too close to that casket. Dead or not, disease is disease, and I ain't takin' my chances getting near it. Just wanted to offer my comforts to Miss Addie." He said the last bit with a mischievous grin.

Stephen gave a harsh laugh. "And she was ready to reject your comforts, small as they are."

The mustached man's face fell hard, but he took a seat next to Stephen, all the same.

They ordered their rounds from Adam the bartender as the old man finished setting a tall glass of musty water and another shorter glass of amber whiskey before the traveler. The man downed the water as the bartender saw to the other two.

For the next couple of hours, the man sat there, drinking his water and then his booze, and then reordering and continuing the cycle. All the while he listened in on Stephen and the mustached man, speaking of things. Of the hard times this country had fallen on. Of wars neither of them had fought in. Of crude jokes and perplexing hyperboles spurred on by their drink. Of women they had slept beside and other such lies. They talked of dead friends and dead enemies; of better days past and darker days ahead; of their hard work and their foolish young hopes; and of all their disillusionments that had since set in. They philosophized and bullshat and cursed on into the late night, and the man listened to it all, growing as drunk as they did with more and more shots. Eventually, Stephen and the mustached man called it a night, paid their dues to Adam, and left the saloon, stumbling and still carrying on.

The man asked where he could find a place to sleep for the night. The bartender grunted that a small inn sat on the northern edge of the town. The man gave a slurred thanks and set his coin down on the bar-top.

He stood up and started to walk on out. But then he recalled the sign he'd seen on the way into town—the one with the town's name that couldn't be read. He turned back about and asked Adam the bartender what town he was even in.

Adam gave what must have been his usual grunt before answering, his back to the man and his attention on sweeping his saloon's floor. "Absolution."

The man had his answer and turned once more to leave. He untied his horse from its spot and pulled it along by the reigns, after an attempt to climb atop it bore no fruit. He slugged through the streets, looking for the inn the bartender had told him of. But the liquor in him and the weariness across his frame made him give up the effort. He found his way to a barn and spent the night sleeping beside his nag, in the hay, along with the other horses and pigs that called the barn home.

When day broke, the man woke with a headache and a start. The memory of where he was and the last evening gradually came back.

He stirred his horse and left the barn before its owner could discover him and raise hell over the sad, drunk stranger who'd had the gall to sleep there. When he walked out into the streets, people were milling about, their day already started.

He saw to resupplying his provisions and filling his canteen, deciding to continue on his way through the state.

Before noon had struck, he had mounted his horse once more and had left Absolution behind him. The rest of Texas awaited him.

Patrick Winters is a graduate of Illinois College in Jacksonville, IL, where he earned a degree in English Literature and Creative Writing. He has been published in the likes of *Sanitarium Magazine*, *Deadman's Tome*, *Trysts of Fate*, and other such titles. A full list of his previous publications may be found at his author's site, if you are so inclined to know: http://wintersauthor.azurewebsites.net/Publications/List

Through Dry Places

Dave Higgins

Orlin rolled out of his saddle just before it dropped from under him. Seemed his horse'd finally gone the way of an honest man in court: staggering along for a while then getting tangled up in itself and falling. Barely mid-morning and the heat already melted the distance. It was times like this he missed the East; good scores were fewer and escapes harder, but you never sweated your drink away before you'd even put the canteen down.

He patted his horse on the nose. Its eyes met his for a moment, then it quivered and stilled. Judgement for the prosecution.

Picking up his derby from the ground, he dusted it off and set it back in place.

A turn on the spot revealed a whole lot of nothing much. No point waiting for a Good Samaritan. On the bright side, he'd almost certainly lost the previous owners of his gold.

Gold that weighed him down but he wasn't finished owning himself. The way things were going, if he left it someone dishonest'd pass near and notice the dead horse. Bury it then? If he spotted a fresh hole, he'd investigate so that had a similar problem. Old holes though... the sort no one'd poke around in even if they noticed it. He untied the first bag of gold and sidled toward the rattler sunning itself on a pile of rocks.

Cold eyes glared at him and a rattle cut the air.

Stopping, he snapped his arm forward and released his hold.

Fangs punched through leather, but didn't stop the bag sliding into the shadows.

A second trip, made harder by not wanting to approach an irritated rattler but not have the bag land short either, added the rest of the gold to the improvised stash.

He unfolded his sketch map and aligned himself as well as he could. Canteen and saddlebags slung over his shoulders and derby pushed down, he trudged on in the direction he'd been riding.

Close on an hour later, something poked up into the oppressive bowl of the sky ahead. After some squinting through the haze, he made out a sort of spire. Must be Stillbellow. It'd worked. He'd almost ended up Orlin jerky. But cutting across'd worked. Even tepid, his celebratory swig of water tasted great.

Reminding himself distances got tricky in the west, he resisted the desire to start running. The added time'd be useful for thinking anyway. Stillbellow was a scratch on a map. So, what was likely to work best on some out-of-the-way townsfolk? Only survivor of an Indian attack? Indians round here weren't known for raiding, and it'd raise questions why he wasn't injured at all. Mustered out and heading home? Might make the horse tricky to explain. Unless he claimed to be an officer; that brought its own problems, though. The sun pressed down harder, opening cracks in each new idea.

Thanking whatever kept the good folks of Stillbellow from ranging wide today, he crested the final rise. Low buildings clustered along two streets with a tall church at the middle. The feeling of wrongness that'd whispered for a while was loud in the silence. He stumbled to a halt. Where was everyone? This wasn't just staying close to home; there was no one. No old men on stoops, no children shouting, no blacksmith hammering, and no animals.

One hand resting on his revolver, he paced closer. Nothing moved apart from the air—and even that was barely noticeable. All the doors were closed and the windows shuttered. Entire place looked tidier than a good suit, and about as cheerful. The rough plank wall snatched at his shirtsleeve as he sidled along it to the crossroads.

The other street was as empty as the first. Thirst bit at his throat, whining for something stronger than water. No sign of a saloon, but there was a general store.

A sprint placed him flat against the boards beside the window. Leaning round, he peered through the gap in the shutters.

Vague shapes in the darkness, too big and still to be people.

After lowering his saddlebags to the ground, he ducked beneath the sill and tested the door. Closed, but not locked.

Revolver drawn, he shoved it open. He dived in as fast, back hitting the inside wall.

Scents of tobacco, liniment, and other normal things drifted over him. Light spilled across clean planks, revealing two counters and several empty shelves

A tense moment later, he eased into the room. This was more than everyone visiting someone's house for a town meeting.

Peering behind the counters, he found a single bottle of root beer in a corner. Must've rolled there when they cleared everything else out. A search of the upstairs discovered the wardrobe empty and the bed stripped. Everything was tidy though. No hint of violence or hurry. He holstered his revolver.

Sugary sassafras flooding his mouth, he strolled to the end of the street, then back. More shuttered houses. If it weren't for the scuffed up dirt and the smells of occupancy, he'd wonder if they'd built the town for people to arrive later.

He paused at the corner. The church door was open a crack. Had he missed it or...?

Either way, it was a better bet for answers than checking a random house. Placing his saddlebags back on the ground, he drew his revolver.

A firm touch swung the door wide enough to see in. A boarded-up window cast the pulpit into shadow but the remaining windows flooded the center of the church with multicolored light. Which made it even more obvious the entire town wasn't gathered in the pews. Slipping through the gap, he headed down the aisle.

Something scuffed to his left.

He spun, thumb pulling the hammer up, as a darker shadow swished past the corner of his eye.

Then jerked his arm up, breath racing, when he saw the collar. "Sorry, reverend."

"Not your fault." Despite his kind words, the priest stayed back, near a tiny doorway that Orlin hadn't noticed until now. "I heard footsteps and hoped you weren't... well. But where are my manners. Jedidiah Clayton."

"Orlin Shelby." Orlin eased the hammer down and holstered his weapon. "Forgive my bluntness, but seems more than manners's gone missing round here."

"The previous incumbent and his followers founded Stillbellow to be a quiet space to follow God. Seemed a promising flock to me. The savages have prejudices, though. One of their heathen priests got them all riled up, seeking to purge this place. Menfolk drove them off when they came riding around. But that priest of theirs is wily. Started lurking out of sight, playing drums and singing songs to their gods. One morning, 'bout a week ago, opened up the church and the entire town was empty."

"Some Indian just disappeared everyone? Why are you still here then?" Orlin sank onto a pew. "I mean, how are you still here even?"

"That savage must've tried his best; reckon his tricks weren't enough, not with me being shepherd to all those folks. Thought about leaving a couple of times, but didn't have the strength to do it on my own. Now you're here though, there's less risk. We'll head off this evening, after the heat's gone."

Orlin nodded. Made perfect sense. This place was empty. The two of them'd be much safer traveling together. "I'll check the town. See if there's anything left worth taking."

"No. Stay and talk... I mean, I've enough supplies here and I've been alone for a week."

He should stay. Find out more about this Indian maybe. The reverend must have gathered everything up already. But his saddlebags... "Right you are. Left my belongings across the street. Just fetch them in and I'll be back."

The reverend nodded. "Doubt you've eaten in a while. I'll put something together."

Orlin tipped his derby, before yanking it off his head and smiling ruefully. Smoothing his hair, he ducked out the door.

A horse whickered in the distance. Maybe Indian magic missed it somehow; or it wandered in after. Or someone else was here. Plenty of ways having a horse made leaving easier. Leaving his saddlebags for the moment, he crept around the church and over to the corner.

An Indian, covered in paint and feathers, skulked along the street, holding a bag and a sort of crude brush. A rifle jutted above one shoulder. Beyond him, a thin horse stood placidly.

Orlin ducked back before he was noticed. Must be that Indian priest the reverend talked about, come to finish what he started. He drew his revolver and eased the hammer up.

The Indian moved into view, eyes fixed on the church.

He might glance around any second now. Bracing his weapon with both hands, Orlin fired.

The Indian spun, blood spraying from his shoulder.

Before his target recovered, Orlin fired twice more.

Gray powder spilled out of the bag as the Indian fell.

Hands shaking, Orlin stumbled closer. Three hits. Three good hits. His opponent was dead. Whatever he'd planned was over. Crouching, he grabbed the barrel of the rifle and yanked it free.

The horse's stance was stiffer, but it showed no sign of bolting yet. After drawing a couple of deep breaths, Orlin strolled toward it.

The horse tilted its head as he approached, then nuzzled his outstretched palm.

Running his fingers along its neck, he moved beside it. Keeping one hand in place, he gripped the saddle with the other. After waiting a moment to be sure the horse was still calm, he swung himself up.

The horse whickered, but settled.

He looked at the church then back along the street. If the Indian'd been doing strange rituals for days, he must have a camp nearby, which meant supplies. He'd promised the reverend he'd— He shook himself. More supplies meant less risk traveling. The reverend'd understand; and wasn't like there was a rush to be gone any more.

He gave his new horse another stroke and set off toward the tallest rise. Should give him the best view of likely places.

More heat and dust.

And enough wagon tracks, hoof treads, and boot scuffs around the end of a narrow fold in the land that even he could make them out. Must be something important to get visited so often. A little voice whispered about seeking the reverend's advice before doing anything rash, but the weight of the sun crushed the idea of riding back and then out again. Besides the threat was dead. He turned his horse down the slope.

Closer to more tracks showed up, spread wide enough that they must have come from all over the town. Something seemed odd about them. Cradling his new rifle, he moved closer to the fold.

The scent of dust thickened in his nostrils. Almost at the mouth, he realized all the boot prints he'd seen faced in one direction. Curiosity warring with the desire to take his horse and head for somewhere far away, he dismounted and moved forward.

A dead man, dried out like he'd been there for weeks, lay in the mouth of the fold. A broad bladed knife jutted from his chest.

As Orlin crept on, he noticed more bodies, men, women, and children by the sizes and clothes. Each bore a single stab wound to the heart, a few with the blade still sticking out. The sight of the first wagon, slaughtered horse between the poles, confirmed his growing fear; these were the townsfolk.

Gravel and dust spurted beneath his boots as he sprinted out of the fold. Leaping into the saddle, he galloped away. No way he was hanging around Stillbellow till dark.

Shouldering the church doors open, he stumbled in. "Reverend. Come on. We need to go."

The reverend stepped through the side door, clutching a candlestick. "I heard shooting. When you didn't come back—"

"That Indian priest came skulking in. I shot him. Took his horse. I..." Orlin sagged against a pew. "I found the townsfolk, too."

"You killed the shaman? I'm finally safe." The reverend lowered his candlestick and grinned. "We need to leave, find people, but there's no rush. Rest a while."

Maybe the reverend had a point. Orlin collapsed onto the pew.

A sharp pain hammered through his temple as the rifle smacked into it. He shot upright. Even if the threat was over, there was no benefit in sitting around. And if it wasn't, waiting just made it worse. "Kind thought. But I'll sleep better with a bunch of miles between me and whatever happened here."

The reverend frowned for a moment, then sighed. "Suppose getting there sooner's got its advantages, too. Mostly packed already anyway."

"You get the last of your stuff while I see what that Indian had on his horse." Orlin paused. What if some evil magic lurked in the Indian's bags? Best to have a bit of Godly protection. The reverend seemed nervous enough about leaving; asking him might put them back where they started. Just dumping them without looking risked losing food and water, though. Then inspiration struck. He strolled toward the pulpit. "Don't want to forget the Good Book, reverend. I'll—"

"No! Leave it alone!"

Orlin spun, one hand already on the Bible. The book shifted, dislodging dust and a pile of papers.

The reverend lurched into the aisle, arm shielding his eyes. "I mean, it will keep this place safe until help returns."

Orlin raised a palm in apology and dropped to a crouch. "I'll just gather up—"

He wasn't a great reader, but one phrase leapt out from the top of the page. *Stillbellow is an anchor to the flesh.* He grabbed more pages. Jagged handwriting, mixed with strange symbols. Angular rather than curving like the ones the Indian'd painted on his skin.

Gnarled fingers tore the paper out of his grip. "I thought we were going. Forget those."

Orlin straightened. His head ached. This wasn't right. Suddenly, the reverend wanted to leave. All the wagons and people; no way he'd have not noticed it them leaving. He'd said this place was promising, so why'd his sermon sound like Stillbellow was a problem. And what kind of preacher let the Good Book get dusty? "Steady on. I reckon there's some things need discussing."

Wild eyes met his. "You're a sinful man, Mr Shelby. I see it in you. I'm offering you a chance to help me. To make yourself useful before you pay for your sins. If you don't want that, then leave."

Orlin yanked his revolver out and stumbled backward. Please let him be wrong. "You killed them all didn't you?"

The reverend tittered. "They killed themselves. All going to Hell now."

Orlin's hand shook, sending his shot wide.

The reverend twisted as Orlin's second shot clipped his left arm.

click

Grin not reaching his eyes, the reverend straightened and stalked closer.

What–? He'd forgotten to reload after killing the Indian.

The rifle! Please let it be loaded. He wrestled with the strap, then swung it up.

The reverend lunged.

Pain hammered into his shoulder. The scent of crude gunpowder cut the dust as the reverend collapsed backward.

Gaze flicking between the rifle and the reverend, Orlin managed to work the bolt. Before he could change his mind, he pulled the trigger again.

Blood, dark in the shadow of the boarded window, oozed away from the reverend's sprawled body.

Orlin staggered across the altar and down the far side of the pews, keeping the rifle tight at his shoulder despite the pain. A glance into the reverend's hidey-hole revealed a plate of dry bread and meat, some scattered papers and clothes, and a sack with enough food and water for one man to reach civilization.

No longer fearing Indian magic, he transferred the supplies and ammunition to his saddlebags, checked his weapons had a full load, and mounted up.

He'd never been a Godly person, but seemed like it might be time for that to change.

After a moment's thought, he turned his horse toward his stash of gold. If he was going to be virtuous, he'd need money to donate.

Dave Higgins writes speculative fiction, often with a dark edge. Despite forays into the mundane worlds of law and IT, he was unable to completely escape the liminal zone between mystery and horror.

Born in the least mystically significant part of Wiltshire, England, and raised by a librarian, he started reading shortly after birth and has not stopped since. He currently lives in Bristol with his wife, Nicola, his cats, Jasper and Una, a plush altar to the Dark Lord Cthulhu, and many shelves of books.

It's rumoured he writes out of a fear that he will otherwise run out of things to read.

Find out more here: https://davehigginspublishing.co.uk

THE AMARILLO JOB

(EXCERPT FROM THE NOVEL, *DEVLIN*)

JEFFREY L. BLEHAR

Saturday 24 July, 1920

I had planned to drive straight through from Santa Fe to Tulsa, stopping only when I needed gasoline for the Roadster. One of the necessary stops turned out to be Amarillo, Texas. It was a cow town, and I wanted to spend as little time there as I could. My plan fell apart almost as soon as I set foot in the dusty town. Amarillo was a place not ready for a man like me, but it turns out I wasn't ready for a town like Amarillo, either.

The dust had been so thick on the way into town, I needed to clean off my windscreen. I pulled into the first gasoline station I came across. It was the outskirts of Amarillo but was a bustle of activity. I paid the attendant to fill the tank, check the oil, and clean the windscreen. While I waited for the teenager to perform his duties, I walked over to the general store across the dusty street. I was hoping to find a pack of Lucky's and a cold cola for my parched throat.

I entered the store and waited for my eyes to adjust to the dim lighting. It was a stark contrast to the bright sunshine outside. The store clerk was helping a young woman with her purchase, so I browsed the store. It was stocked to the brim with anything a rancher and his family would need. Canned goods filled the shelves along one wall. Fabric of many varieties lined another wall. Signs advertising feed, straw, and fencing materials were hung on the far wall. Kitchen utensils, and dry goods filled displays spread out over the salesfloor.

"What do you mean you can't extend my credit?" I overheard the young woman ask the clerk.

"I'm sorry, but I can't allow you goods on credit anymore," the clerk responded in a sympathetic tone.

"We have always bought on credit and paid it off at the end of every month. You know Double O Ranch will pay off the debt next week," she explained.

"I know, but it is the new store policy. The new owners have expressly ordered us not to accept credit from the small ranches anymore," the clerk explained.

"New owners?" she asked.

"Sorry ma'am, but the Wilson Feed and General Store is now the property of Kelvin Johnson and he doesn't want to extend credit to ranchers."

"Kelvin Johnson doesn't want to extend credit to us, because we are his only competition left!" the woman said, raising her voice. "KJ Ranch has swallowed up all the family ranches on the Llano Estacado, except for us. He wants our grassland and is trying to drive us out..."

I continued to listen as I pretended to examine some baking tins. It was none of my concern, and I should have let it be, but there was something about this strong-willed young woman.

The clerk looked unsettled by the exchange and lowered his voice. "You should just sell to him. There is a reason you are the last remaining hold-outs. He gets what he wants, no matter who he hurts."

The woman did not keep her voice low but raised it even more. "My family broke that land. We have worked that land for four generations and I will be damned if the Double O fails on my watch!"

She glared at the clerk. He was visibly shaken but held his ground. "If you have cash, we can sell you anything you want. Even Kelvin Johnson wouldn't be so bold as to risk the outrage over turning away honest currency. Don't you have the cash?"

"You know we don't. We won't have it for a week, when Simpson returns from Dallas with the profits from the market," she explained.

The clerk shrugged. "Come back in a week, then."

The raven-haired woman stormed off, out of the store. I had already made my decision to hang around Amarillo for a few days. I knew there would be no dough for me in my new venture, but I knew I could sort this mess out for the Double O.

I picked up a few packs of Lucky's, and bought myself a pair of dungarees, work shirt, and a pair of boots. I figured, if I was going to stick around Amarillo, I had better dress the part. My suit and wingtips were going to stick out a little too much for my liking.

I knew better than to ask the clerk anything. I wasn't going to get any straight dope from a KJ employee. The teenage gas attendant would be a better source of information.

I lighted a Lucky and walked back across the street to my Roadster. The attendant was just finishing cleaning the screen when I approached.

"What do I owe you?" I asked.

"You was running on empty, so it's two dollars for the gasoline. The rest was complimentary," he answered.

I handed him a fiver.

"I got change in the station. Be right back," he muttered.

"Wait a second, kid," I said. "You can keep the whole fiver if you answer me a few questions."

His eyes lit up. "What you need to know, mister?"

"Tell me about the Double O ranch."

"Sure thing. It is a small ranch out on the Llano Estacado. Been here almost as long as anybody else. Owen O'Dea started her up and passed her down to his son. Now it's run by Cait O'Dea, and she's something!" he explained.

"I know, I just saw her almost take a clerk's head off across the street," I explained.

"Oh. She's been under a lot of pressure lately. She's been running the ranch on her own since her daddy died. She hasn't even married to have a husband or sons help her with the place."

"She has no help?" I asked, astonished.

He smiled. "Well, she had Danny Simpson, who is the ranch foreman and a few ranch-hands, but not enough. KJ has hired most men away. The only ones that stayed were the ones most loyal to her daddy."

I saw my way in to asking about the big man and took it. "Who is KJ?" I asked feigning ignorance.

"Who is KJ? Mister, you must be from out of town," he said, exasperated.

"Oh, more than you know. Now, tell me about him," I demanded.

"Mr. Johnson owns the largest ranch on the Llano Estacado. Matter of fact, the Double O is the only other ranch left in these parts. The KJ Ranch is so big, they say it takes a week just to ride across. I don't know if that's true, but it may as well be. He is a man you don't cross. He owns everything around these parts, including this service station and that general store across the way."

"I take it, he isn't the type of man one tells 'no'?" I asked.

"No sir! Only Ailbe O'Dea ever said no to Mr. Johnson and his headstrong daughter has taken after her old man," he said.

"Thanks," I muttered. "The change is yours. You earned it."

"Anytime you need information, you come ask for Don," he said.

"Just Don?" I asked.

"Everyone knows me around here," he explained.

I smiled at the young attendant's cockiness. "Sure thing, kid."

I jumped in my Roadster and headed into Amarillo proper to find lodgings for the night. I needed to find a way to introduce myself to Ms. O'Dea.

I had spent the night in some rundown roadside motel. I didn't think the mugs from Denver on my tail would've thought to search Amarillo, but I kept my Roadster out of sight, just in case.

I was wearing my new get up. I must admit, I didn't feel at home in the new rags. The ranching cowhand life was not for me. I was still at a loss as to how a city slicker like me was going to fool Cait O'Dea into thinking I was an experienced ranch hand. There was no way that was going to happen.

I also knew I wouldn't be able to fool Johnson and hook up with his spread. I had to find a way to make sure the Double O Ranch was out from under KJ's thumb, and make sure it stayed that way after I blew town, all while fooling experienced cowmen that I was one of them. I should have just forgotten the whole mess and moved on, as I originally intended.

I followed the directions I received to the Double O. It was easy enough —miles upon miles of fenced in grazing lands with thousands upon thousands of cattle. I was clearly passing through KJ territory.

I found the dirt road turnoff and took it. My Roadster barreled down the dirt road, leaving an ominous cloud of dust in my wake. There would be no subtle entry to the ranch.

I tried to memorize the layout of the buildings as I approached the ranch. There were several barns, a corral, stables for the horses, a bunkhouse for the men, more than a few scattered outbuildings for tools and supplies, and the main ranch house. This is where I would try my luck.

My Roadster ground to a halt some yards from the house. I didn't want to cause alarm by pulling right up to the front porch. I exited the relative safety of my automobile and headed for the house. I kept a leisurely pace as I took notice of several ranch-hands making their presence known.

As I reached the sole step leading to the large wrap-around porch, the door opened. There was Cait O'Dea in all her ferocious beauty, Winchester rifle in hand.

My eyes surveyed the rifle in her arms. The weapon had speed, accuracy, and distance—an impressive weapon, even if a touch outdated. I noticed the rifle was loaded and primed for action. The rifle was not for show—Ms. O'Dea meant business.

"Can I help you, stranger?" She asked. Her voice full of suspicion.

I had left my Browning in the auto and was feeling a touch naked at the moment. O'Dea's Winchester and half a dozen tough ranch-hands left me feeling exposed. "I came to offer my services."

She looked me up and down and tried to stifle a laugh. "Got a lot of ranching experience, do ya?"

"Not a lick," I responded. There was no way I was going to fool her, so I took a different tack.

"Ain't got much use for anything else," she said, squinting her eyes at me.

I could tell she was trying to figure me out. "I couldn't help but overhear your conversation with the store clerk at the feed store yesterday. I came to try to help."

She finally lowered her rifle. "I appreciate that, Mr. —"

"Devlin," I added.

"I appreciate it Mr. Devlin, but that's my and KJ business. It's of no concern of yours. Now, I'd appreciate it if you'd get off my property," she responded in a steely curt manner.

"Sorry, ma'am, but I made it my business. I didn't come here to ask you for anything. I came to tell you I'm doing this thing and you'd be wise to keep yourself and your men out of my way until I'm done," I threatened. I then turned and returned to my Roadster. I pulled away and left the way I had come. Ms. O'Dea was still standing on the porch as I beat a path out of sight.

My next stop was to pay Johnson a visit. I decided to give him the chance to back away from his attempts to overtake the Double O Ranch. Based on past experiences, I knew a man like Johnson wouldn't take me seriously, but he, like all the others would regret that decision.

I knew my luck wasn't going to hold out forever and blowing a tire out on the desolate road to KJ Ranch was the line. I had a spare, but I didn't like being out in the open like this. I set to work changing the tire, trying to keep my eyes open for anyone approaching on the road.

While concentrating on the tire and the road, I neglected the grazing land on either side of the road. KJ grazing land. While my back was turned, working on removing the bad tire, I heard the snorting of a horse. I spun and was on my feet in a flash. I found myself looking up at three riders— only a barbed-wire fence separating me from them. I had removed my coat while I changed the tire in the hot sun, leaving my Browning exposed to the men.

"Howdy," the leader said as he scanned the vicinity to make sure I was alone.

I wiped my brow with a handkerchief. "Afternoon," I responded, taking note of the Colt forty-five revolvers lashed to each man's hip. Each had the butt of a rifle sticking out of a saddle holster. These men were armed for a range war.

"Can I help you?" The leader asked, pretending not to notice my shoulder holster.

"Maybe," I answered. "Is this the road to KJ Ranch?"

He nodded in the affirmative. His eyes were clear and focused. This was not a man to tangle with if it could be avoided. I turned my attention to the two other riders. One was older, but a coldness from years of experience hinted at a ruthless streak. The other was just as dangerous. He was young, and fidgety. He was itching to make his bones with these boys. I wasn't eager to turn my back on any of these snakes.

"I have business with Mr. Johnson," I declared.

The leader held my gaze and didn't blink. "Is that so?"

The youngest of the riders interrupted our stare-down. "Fella's got a pretty fancy piece, Oscar."

"I seen it, Danny...now hush your lips," the leader said, without removing his eyes from mine.

"Just looking for some work," I said.

"We got no need of some fancy city gunman out here," he answered.

"Jus' kill 'im and be done with this nonsense," the older rider muttered, looking into the sky.

"That's not necessary," I said. "I'll just fix my auto and be on my way."

"Oscar, we should take that piece and his auto. Let him walk back to town," the young rider suggested.

"Jus' kill 'im and be on our way. I'm tired of being in this damned saddle all day," the old man stated.

The headman's eyes still hadn't broken with mine. I had a shotgun in the trunk, but that would do me no good. I had my little twenty-two resting in

158

the front seat. I could probably get to it and get a shot off, but that would only knock the man from his horse. From this distance, the damage it would do would just piss the rider off. If I went for the Browning, I would have three bullets in me before I had it out, let alone aimed. I was at their mercy.

The leader finally broke the silence. "Nah. Boss don't want any unwanted attention right now. We don't need no Pinkertons to come looking for this fella if he goes missing."

"Looks like your lucky day, mister," the young rider added.

The old man grunted something under his breath.

"Be on your way and don't let me see you 'round here again. Get it?" Oscar said.

I nodded. I waited for them to back away before I returned to my work. I breathed a large sigh once they were out of range. They holed up and waited in the distance to make sure I completed my repairs and turned back the way I had come. That was the roughest spot I had been in since the war.

I had a feeling Johnson was planning something major soon. He didn't want any outside authorities poking around Amarillo. That's why they couldn't take a chance rubbing me out. They didn't know who would come looking for me. My gut told me Johnson was going to make his move on the Double O sooner rather than later.

I didn't know what they were planning, but the pit in my stomach told me it would probably be violent and ugly for O'Dea and her men. Just a cursory glance of her men the day before told me they stood no chance against the trained guns of KJ. I had to warn them...or, at least try.

I arrived back at the Double O Ranch as the sun was setting in the western sky. Cait O'Dea was back at the door with Winchester in hand.

I pulled the Roadster up to the porch, this time and exited with little concern for my well-being. I wasn't sure how much time I had to convince her of the danger she was in. It was days at the most; hours at the least. It would turn out I was wrong on both counts.

"I thought I told you to get off my property," Ms. O'Dea spurted, her annoyance shining through.

"You have to listen to me for a minute," I uttered as I approached the porch.

She raised the rifle to eye level. Staring down the barrel of a rifle is never a comforting thing. "Hold it right there," she ordered.

"Johnson and his boys are coming for you," I responded.

She smirked. "He wouldn't be so bold as to forcibly take the Double O in a firefight."

"You're wrong. He has some plan that requires he possess your land sooner than later," I said.

I could tell from the expression on her face, I wasn't getting anywhere. I saw movement from the corner of my eyes. Several of O'Dea's men had come up behind me, hands resting on their hips. All armed with revolvers.

I tried to think of something to say to convince the hardheaded woman when a horse galloped up to the ranch house. A man, slouched in the saddle fell to the ground with a loud groan.

The men and O'Dea rushed to his side. I could see the man was gut-shot.

"Help me get him inside," O'Dea ordered her men. "Wilson, you keep an eye on our friend, here. Roger, you ride out to the doc...fast as you can!"

"Wait," I interjected. "This is Johnson making his move. You send anyone out to get help and they ain't coming back."

160

A look of panic crossed her face, then she steeled her nerve. "How do I know it wasn't you that done this?"

"What do I have to gain?" I asked.

"I don't know, but you wait here, while we get Johnny inside and stop the bleeding."

I nodded. Johnny was a dead man, but I didn't think my observation would be warmly received at the moment, so I kept it to myself.

I waited while they dealt with the wounded man. Wilson kept his rifle trained on me. He had a nervous look about him, which in turn made me nervous. All I needed right now was for Wilson to get spooked and squeeze of a shot out of panic.

After what seemed an eternity, Cait O'Dea returned. "Looks like you are off the hook. Johnny says it was KJ men that ambushed him as he was fixin' a post at the edge of my land.

"If they are coming for us, it looks like you just threw your lot in with us. That's the only road in or out of here and I don't think your auto will make it across the open cattle land."

"I went over to my Roadster, opened the trunk and pulled out my shotgun and all the shells I had left. I then grabbed my twenty-two from under the driver seat. It wasn't going to do much, but you never knew when you might need it.

O'Dea's brow furrowed. "Who are you, exactly?"

"Johnson's nightmare," I said as I scoped out the area.

"I need your best shot with a rifle, there in the hayloft. Maybe pick a few off before they get to the ranch. Hopefully, they won't realize Johnny made it back with a warning."

"That's me," O'Dea said.

"You're the best shot with a rifle?" I asked.

"Yes...does that surprise you?"

I shrugged. "Nothing about you would surprise me right now. I need the next best man with a rifle in the second-floor window of the house."

"That's Dooley," she answered and nodded at the man, I assumed was Dooley. The man bolted for the house.

That left Wilson, Roger and two men whose names I didn't know.

"Alright, I said. Roger, I need you on the first floor of the barn. You have to keep anyone from getting up into the hayloft. We need Ms. O'Dea protected. She will be the only one who can cover the entire area. If she goes down, it's all over. Understand?"

"Yes," Roger uttered and headed toward the barn.

"Wilson and you two, man the windows on the first floor of the house. I need two facing this way and one covering the rear. Don't forget to keep up with your flanks. We can't have anyone sneaking up along the side, understand?" I asked.

"We got it," Wilson said, and the three men left to take up their positions.

Cait O'Dea had maintained a tough exterior while her men were present, but that started to slip once it was just she and I. I needed her to focus and stay tough. "You can do this. Being a woman and running a ranch is a lot more difficult than this," I lied.

The resolve returned to her face and she nodded.

"Remember, no matter what happens, you stay in that loft. We aren't all going to get out of this alive. You must accept that right now. You can't risk everyone by trying to save everyone. Stay focused on KJ men and the others will do the same," I instructed. "Now, go get in place."

"Where are you going to be for all this?" she asked, showing a surprising amount of concern for someone she had just met.

"Trying to buy you a little more time," I said turning away from her.

I got in my Roadster and began driving away from the ranch. I had the shotgun in my lap, dropped the twenty-two in my jacket pocket and set

162

the Browning on the seat next to me. I took slow, even breaths as I rushed away toward an unknown number of cowboys heading my way.

I sped down the dirt road. It was the easiest way into and out of the Double O. I figured the cowboys would use the road until they got near the ranch and then they'd split off to surround the place. Once I decided I was far enough out, I pulled a u-turn and put the Roadster in park, right in the middle of the road.

I left the driver door open and her engine humming, while I hid in the brush with shotgun in hand. I waited, sweat running down my forehead. I hoped the gang would send a scout ahead of the main party to make sure the way was clear. If they decided against this strategy and all came in one way, I was finished before I ever got started.

After several minutes waiting in the quiet night air, I saw some movement further up the road, cautiously moving toward me, on the road. I was in luck—it was a lone rider. I knew the others would be close behind, but this gave me the opportunity to take one of the bastards out and put some fear into the rest of them.

The dark figure approached. It was a single rider on horseback. I prepared myself to take the first free shot I had. The rider climbed down from his mount to examine the still running Roadster.

He held his mount's reigns in his hand as he approached, Colt forty-five revolver in the other hand. I saw a rifle stock sticking out of a saddle holster. I could use that rifle. I waited a second longer and recognized the man's face in the moonlight. It was that obnoxious kid, Danny.

I knew this was the best chance I was going to get. I wanted him to square-up for my shot, so I called out in the night. "Danny," I whispered loud enough for him to hear me.

He turned toward me upon hearing his name. I stood and unloaded the shotgun into his chest. He stumbled back and fell against the side of the automobile. The horse bucked at the noise of the blast but held its ground—someone had trained her well. I reached the horse and pulled the rifle free of its sheath—a fully loaded Remington repeater.

The shotgun blast had alerted the rest of the gang and I could hear the thunder of horse hooves approaching. I stood on the hood of the Roadster to take aim into the darkness. I steeled my nerve and waited until I could make out a line of horses galloping right at me. I squeezed off a shot and saw a rider go down. The cowboys broke ranks and sought cover in the scrub-brush lining the dirt road.

They were still coming, but I had slowed them for a few moments. I squeezed off two more shots from the rifle, knowing I hit only air. I wanted them to think I was still trying to pick them off in the brush. I slid off the hood of the auto and was behind the wheel before I heard their first shots. I sped off back toward the ranch.

I pulled the roadster into the barn and hoped Roger wouldn't panic and blast me. He seemed cool and collected. I nodded to him and he returned the nod. I climbed the ladder to the hayloft where Ms. O'Dea was waiting.

"Twenty would be my guess," I said in way of greeting.

"That's all?" Her response dripped with sarcasm. "Twenty against seven... piece of cake."

"I got two and bought us a bit more time," I said, ignoring her flippant tone. I knew this was just her way of masking her fear. I'll take sarcastic over hysterical any day.

We waited what seemed an eternity. A rifle shot echoed out into the night. It had come from the house, but I couldn't see any movement from my location. I figured it was just a scaredy shot from one of O'Dea's boys in the house.

Several minutes later I saw movement on the far side of the property. It looked like six or seven men, on foot trying to circle around the house. They were too far away for O'Dea or I to plug them. It didn't look like the boys in the house had seen them yet. I knew this meant there were more than likely six or seven working their way around the back side of the barn we were in.

I yelled down to Roger. "They're coming...keep an eye on the tree-line behind us."

"Got it," Roger yelled in response.

I climbed down the ladder to my Roadster, grabbed the shotgun and opened the front door of the barn enough to slide the shotgun through. It wouldn't do anyone any damage, but it might alert the boys in the house to the men slinking along their flank. I pulled the trigger and the shotgun blast briefly filled the night.

Then, all hell broke loose. I shut the door and barricaded it. Rifle and gun fire filled the night. Roger was laying it on thick out the back of the barn. I could hear O'Dea's rifle ring out several times above me. Most of the gunfire was coming from the area of the house.

I climbed back into the hayloft to get a better sense of our situation. Three men lay still in the corral. Cait O'Dea had caught them trying to sneak through, using the Double O's horses as cover. It didn't work. O'Dea hadn't lied, she was a crack shot with that Winchester.

Dooley had three or four of them pinned down by the tool shed. Wilson was covering the front of the house, but the other two fellows must have been having a hellacious time around the back of the house. Gunfire obliterated the silent night.

I knew Roger could use my help, so I decided to go back down to the ground level. Just as I was about to make my move, I saw a panicked Wilson disappear from sight. My guess was the two boys needed help. The focus of the gun battle appeared to have shifted to the back of the house. I hadn't prepared for that.

As I reformulated a plan, Wilson returned to his post, bloodied, but alive. I wasn't sure if it was his blood, but they needed help.

"Keep them away from the left side of the house," I ordered O'Dea.

"What are you planning?" she asked.

"Probably the dumbest thing I've done in a while," I answered.

"Well, at least it ain't the dumbest thing you ever done," she replied, sarcasm still masking fear.

"You shoulda seen me in the war."

"You'll have to tell me that story sometime."

I smiled and disappeared down the ladder. I reloaded Roger's cache of revolvers, handed him the rifle I borrowed from Danny, and slapped him on the shoulder. I wasn't very good at pep-talks, but I think he got my point.

I opened the front door of the barn and slid through, leaving myself completely exposed. I trusted Cait O'Dea and Dooley to keep me covered. I ran to the house. The left side had been protected by O'Dea from her perch in the hayloft. I was in the clear until I rounded the back. I had my Browning in hand as I crept into position.

I knew we had to push the offensive. The longer the battle raged, the worse for us. We were dug in, but limited on ammunition. They came for battle, we did not.

I was able to take stock of the situation behind the house without being detected. I counted four dead cowboys and about six more throwing lead from good positions in the yard.

I had a good angle on one of them behind an outhouse. If I took the shot, I would expose my position. I decided one more dead cowboy was worth it, especially seeing as it was the old man who seemed intent on killing me earlier.

I aimed, fired and watched as the shot blew his hat off his head.

He slouched to the ground with a new bullet-hole where his ear had been.

The shot had drawn the attention of the other cowboys, who opened fire on my position. I darted back around the side of the house to relative safety. I crept toward the front of the house to see how Dooley and Wilson were managing the riders they had pinned down.

I saw one dead cowboy and two more still firing on the front of the house. Dooley was trading shots with the duo, but I saw no signs of Wilson.

I found myself taking cover behind an old rain barrel. An idea sprung into my head...not a good idea, but an idea nonetheless.

I turned the rain barrel on its side, which took a surprising amount of effort. The water rushed across the parched dust. I then rolled the barrel out into the middle of the fracas. It drew the attention of the two cowboys and they opened fire on the barrel. This left them exposed to O'Dea in the hayloft. She didn't miss her opportunity and downed both in rapid succession.

I made it to the front porch and crashed through an already shattered window. I found my way to the front door to find Wilson already dead on the floor.

I didn't want Dooley to plug me, so I warned him of my presence. "Dooley, it's Devlin...don't shoot me."

"Okay," was his only response.

"O'Dea has the front covered. Get down here and help with the crums out the back."

"Got it," he said. He was a man of few words.

I heard him clomping down the stairs, but I took off through the front door to check on the others in the barn. As I ran along the front of the house, a shot whizzed by my head and I fell flat into the dust—Browning falling from my grip. I looked up to see Cait O'Dea taking aim at me. My stomach soured and then I saw her pointing behind me.

167

A cowboy had managed to cross the front yard and was blocked from O'Dea's line of fire. He was taking aim when O'Dea had shot at me to save my life. I'd have to remember to thank her later.

I rolled toward the porch. My rod out of reach. The porch ledge was protecting me for the time being, but if I moved I was done for. I looked to the hayloft and saw O'Dea was gone. This was a bad sign. The only reason for her to abandon her post was if Roger was dead or wounded.

The cowboy who had me pinned down seemed to know my cover was gone and I heard his boots on the porch walking toward me. I had to think quick.

"You should have gotten out of town when you had the chance, city boy," the cowboy said as he approached.

I recognized the voice as he spoke. It was Oscar, that cold-eyed son of a bitch I had tangled with earlier.

He continued speaking as he approached. "Mr. Johnson always gets what he wants."

My mind raced, searching for a way out of this. He would be standing over me in a few more seconds. Then, a calm came over me and a realization dawned on me...

Oscar arrived, Colt in hand and peered over the edge of the porch only to be welcomed with a face full of lead. He stumbled back and fell against the house, dead. I had forgotten that I had stashed my little twenty-two in my coat pocket. I exhaled deeply, only then realizing I had been holding my breath.

I was done with this fire-fight. I retrieved my Browning and ran into the house. I found Dooley sheltered against the wall as shots filled the entryway. O'Dea's other two men, whose names I never bothered to learn were dead in the doorway. It was Dooley and me against the two remaining cowboys out back by the outhouse. I liked these odds much better. I belly-crawled over to Dooley.

"Take that Winchester you got and get over to that window in the kitchen. It should give you a good angle on those last two crums," I ordered.

He shook his head. "Already tried that. They's dug in like ticks on a hound."

"They won't be for long. When you get a shot, don't miss..."

He nodded and crawled away from me. I gave him a few moments to get into position, before making my move. I loaded the Browning, got ahold of one of the dead men's Colts and reloaded it, as well. I shoved the Colt in my belt and took three long breaths.

I was pretty sure this was the stupid antic that was going to get me killed. My luck had to run out sometime. I stood and heaved myself out the door, right into the line of fire. I dove off the porch and hit the ground hard. The two cowboys now needed to readjust their positions to get an angle on me. I let loose a shot from my Browning, taking one of the gang out. I heard a near simultaneous shot and hoped it was Dooley plugging the other.

I knew I was in the clear when I heard a shout of what I can only assume was triumph coming from Dooley in the house. I got to my feet knowing the battle wasn't won yet. We still had the skirmish at the barn to deal with.

I didn't wait for Dooley, but took off running for the barn. I hoped he would follow, but O'Dea and Roger didn't have time for us to re-group first.

A chill overcame me as I ran for the barn when I failed to hear any gunfire. I froze at the door to the barn. I tried to listen for any signs letting me know who won the skirmish, but all I could hear was my own heart beating in my ears.

I had to know what went down. I opened the door and crept into the dark barn. As I crossed the barn I saw Cait O'Dea walking toward me, supporting the wounded Roger. He looked to be in a bad sort, but he was conscious, and on his feet, even if with O'Dea's help.

We met in the middle of the barn. The whole battle had lasted less than fifteen minutes. We were dead exhausted, but still not done. We still had Johnson to deal with. The Double O wouldn't be safe until he was out of the picture for good.

"Roger's hurt pretty bad. What of the others?" O'Dea asked.

Dooley came bounding through the barn door as I answered. "Three dead in the house. We're the only ones that made it."

A tear formed in Cait's eye. She let it run down her face as she supported Roger with one arm and clenched her Winchester in the other.

"You two need to get Roger to the Doctor. I'll take care of old KJ," I said.

"Dooley can take Roger, I'm coming with you," she responded.

"Can't," I said.

"This is my land, my ranch, and my family honor. I deserve the right to see this finished," she said, steel running through her veins.

"I understand that, but it's the wrong play. The law will understand all the dead cowboys on your land. You have every right to defend what's yours, but I plan on killing Johnson at his place. That is out and out murder. The law will look to you first and if you are in town at the hospital with Roger and Dooley, then you'll have a solid alibi," I explained.

She was angry, but seemed to understand the wisdom of my plan. "How can we ever repay you? Will we see you again?" She asked as Dooley helped Roger onto a wagon bed.

"No repayment needed. No, you'll never see me again. I plan on rubbing Johnson out and then heading east. I got someplace I need to be," I explained.

"Well, thank you for everything," she said in all sincerity as she hugged me close and tight. It caught me off-guard, but I soon returned the hug. As we stood in that bloody, exhausted embrace I couldn't help but think what might have been, under different circumstances.

I broke the embrace, smiled and made for my Roadster. As I peeled away from the Double O Ranch for the last time, O'Dea and Dooley were hitching a horse team up to the wagon to get Roger into town.

As I sped along the lonely dirt roads toward my appointment with Kelvin Johnson, I couldn't help but wonder why he had made his move now. Everything pointed to a rushed job.

A night raid was a good plan, but the night was all wrong. It was not a full-moon, but a gibbous moon was not much better. They would have been in a much better position on a night with a new moon—really shield their approach.

The secretive hints dropped when the three gunmen got the drop on me also gave me pause. They knew something big was up and didn't want me gumming up the works.

Johnson was up to something and needed the Double O now and was willing to face the backlash of slaughtering the ranchers. Johnson owned the town and I was sure the Cheyenne or the Arapaho would take the fall for his bloody ambitions.

The KJ Ranch was enormous, largest in the panhandle, so I was told earlier. It took more time than I expected to cross the lands to the ranch house at the center of Johnson's cattle empire. I hoped the place would be lightly guarded. I knew he sent the majority of his muscle to the Double O and some had to be out on legitimate ranch business, but I couldn't guess who would be at the house.

I left the Roadster as close to the compound as I could without drawing attention. It was a massive system of bunkhouses, stables, corrals, and outbuildings. The house itself was a massive Colonial-styled mansion. Beautiful and completely out of place way out here in cow country. Johnson may have been a lot of things to a lot of people, but subtle he sure wasn't.

I kept to the shadows of the various buildings as I crept toward the house. The place seemed abandoned, and I would have thought Johnson was away, except for the lights burning in the mansion.

I covered the ground to the house without being discovered. This was too easy. Surely, he had spared a few men to watch the homestead.

I circled around the house, figuring the rear entrance was the best way to go. I crept up the three steps to the porch and still had heard nothing. Browning in hand, I reached for the door knob. Before I could reach it, I saw it start to turn. I hid myself against the wall, out of sight from the door. I needed to get the drop on whoever was coming through the door.

I gripped the Browning by the short nose, so I could use it as a club. I held my breath as the door opened. I would have the perfect opportunity to take down whomever it was coming.

I saw movement as a body walked through the door and I swung my rod without hesitation. The blow landed solidly, knocking an old black woman to the ground. I rolled her over to make sure she was still breathing. She was.

She was a cook or a servant of some sort. I felt bad for sapping an innocent old woman, but she was better off sleeping through this whole ordeal.

I listened for any sounds as I entered the house. I searched room by room until I happened on Johnson's office. He was nowhere to be found, but I was finally able to answer the questions which had been bothering me since the assault had started.

Johnson had a topographic map of the entire region built on a table in the corner. The difference is that there was a railroad which didn't exist on the map. It was so clear looking at the topography from a distance. A railroad going through this stretch would be made quicker and cheaper if it could go through the relatively flat land occupied by the Double O Ranch. There were other possible routes, but those would require bridging ravines and streams.

On the desk, I found the signed contract for Western Railroad. Johnson had sold land that wasn't his to a railroad company which was jumping the gun on privatization. The railroads had been nationalized during the war and they would soon be turned over to private companies. So, Johnson needed Cait O'Dea gone before surveyors showed up to start mapping the new route from Phoenix to Tulsa, with a nice big new station in Amarillo. It would be a goldmine if Johnson could pull it off.

Being the richest man in the Texas panhandle wasn't enough for Johnson, he wanted to be the richest man in the southwest. I wasn't going to let this louse walk all over the people of Amarillo, just so he could make even more dough than he already had.

I made sure the rest of the first floor was empty before creeping up to the second floor. The huge French-doors gave away which room was the master bedroom. I tried the knob—locked.

French-doors may have been a fancy rarity out here, but they were no good for security. They buckled quickly under a determined assailant. I planted my left leg and kicked the doors, right where the two met.

The man himself had been reading peacefully in bed when I interrupted him.

He was frozen with fear and indecision. There was little he could do, I had him. He dropped his book and looked around the room for something to help him out of this predicament.

"Do you know who I am?" he asked with an arrogant tone, which was absurd given the situation.

I didn't answer—I put a bullet in his chest and another in his head. I left the way I had come.

Cait O'Dea could now live her life without the fear of getting squeezed out by KJ, and they couldn't pin his murder on her either.

Being around O'Dea and her men reminded me of the camaraderie of war. It made me miss the friendships forged over the threat of death. My old Sergeant had settled down to start a new life in Tulsa. It seemed as good a place as any to lay low for a few days and figure out my next step. I just hoped he had a paying gig for me.

Jeffrey L. Blehar is the author of the *Books of the Broken* series, including *Nighthawks* and *Devlin*. His short stories have appeared in a number of collections and magazines.

Find out more at: https://millhavenpress.com/

CPSIA information can be obtained
at www.ICGtesting.com
Printed in the USA
LVHW111541310519
619751LV00001BA/204/P

9 781912 674039